# IT WAS ALL PART
# OF THE PLAN . . .

"Don't!" Megan screamed, covering her face. What good would it do to hide her face? He'd still photograph her body, her image, placing it on the negative, doing the damage he had designed the camera to do.

"Leave me alone. You've already killed. It's not a disease, it's *you* . . . somehow, it's you."

"That's why I've waited for you. You're interfering with my plan, Megan."

"What plan? Why are you doing this?"

No answer. Just the tiny smile . . .

*Other Avon Flare Books by*
**Barbara Steiner**

THE DREAMSTALKER
NIGHT CRIES
THE PHOTOGRAPHER II: THE DARK ROOM

# the Photographer

## BARBARA STEINER

AN AVON  FLARE BOOK

For Karen Kloverstrom,
my traveling buddy

THE PHOTOGRAPHER is an original publication of Avon Books. This work has never before appeared in book form.

AVON BOOKS
A division of
The Hearst Corporation
1350 Avenue of the Americas
New York, New York 10019

First Avon Flare Printing: October 1989

AVON FLARE TRADEMARK REG. U.S. PAT. OFF. AND IN OTHER COUNTRIES, MARCA REGISTRADA, HECHO EN U.S.A.

Printed in the U.S.A.

K-R 10 9 8 7 6 5 4 3

# Chapter 1

"Cynthia, wait up!" Megan Davidson shouted to her best friend. It was unlike Cynthia to be running down the hall at school. Floating was a better description of the way Cynthia Harlow usually moved. "Are you that hungry?" Megan practically had to grab Cynthia's arm to stop her.

"Oh, Megan, is he gone?" Cynthia looked ready to cry.

"Is who gone? What's the matter, Cyn?"

"Derrick Ames is what's the matter." Cynthia crumpled into a corner near the lunchroom. "He gives me the creeps, Megan. No, that's not right. He scares me."

"Let me get this straight." Megan hid a grin. "Derrick Ames, Derrick with the wire glasses and the kinky hair and brains. The new kid in town? That Derrick scared you? So now you're running down the hall, escaping the dire consequences of his looking at you?" Megan knew her friend Cynthia was often overly dramatic. Megan enjoyed Cynthia's shows, since she herself didn't have an ounce of drama in her body. But this was too much.

"He didn't just look at me, Megan. He's been staring at me ever since he entered Boulder High.

1

I've almost gotten used to that. Or at least I've been able to ignore it. But today he asked me to go to the Homecoming Dance with him.''

"Derrick Ames asked you to go to the Homecoming Dance?''

The idea of Derrick asking any girl to go out amazed Megan. The minute he arrived on the scene, Megan had labeled him a super nerd. A guy who had never dated, and maybe didn't even care. But she'd always had a soft spot in her heart for nerds, underdogs, people who marched to a different drummer. Megan had become friendly with Derrick as soon as he joined the annual and the newspaper staffs. Not male-female friendly, but friendly as in I-have-to-work-with-you, as in I'll-make-the-best-of-it. She couldn't say she liked Derrick yet. He puzzled her. But she certainly admired his work.

"Can't you hear? Take the cotton out of your ears and tell me what to do.'' Anger gave Cynthia some backbone, and she started toward a table in the lunchroom.

Megan followed. "What do you mean, tell you what to do? Did you accept?''

"Of course not. But I was so floored I didn't say anything. He acted as if my silence was a yes. Just because he limits his conversations to ten words, doesn't mean other people do the same.''

Megan pictured the scene: Derrick—short, homely—asking out Cynthia—tall, blond beauty, Homecoming Queen. Cynthia, standing with her mouth open. Derrick, turning and walking away, the date settled in his mind. Megan tried not to giggle.

"It's not funny.'' Cynthia slammed her lunch sack onto the table. "The whole school knows I broke up with Gus last week, so I couldn't say I had a date.''

Cynthia and Gus had provided a lot of people entertainment by having a super-great fight at What's Up, the restaurant on the downtown mall. It was where everyone from school hung out after football games, so there were dozens of witnesses. The event couldn't have gotten more attention if Megan had written it up in headlines for the school newspaper.

"Maybe you can tell him you are half-dead of a broken heart," Megan advised, peering into her brown bag, then pulling out a ham-and-cheese sandwich, potato chips, an apple, and a foil-wrapped slice of German chocolate cake. Her lunch was in sharp contrast with Cynthia's cottage cheese, veggies, and fruit. "Tell him you've sworn off men forever. I'm sure you'll think of something."

"You aren't even sympathetic." Cynthia turned her anger toward Megan, but Megan knew she wasn't really mad at her. "Some friend you are. You probably put him up to it. You've been hanging around him enough. How can you stand him? And why didn't he ask you?"

"He probably doesn't consider me a girl, since he works with me. Derrick's okay. A little weird, but all talented, creative people are a little strange. I'm in shock, though, about his asking you out. You and Derrick Ames. Wow, that's news. I think I'll write an article for next week's paper about odd couples in Boulder High."

"Megan, you're disgusting. Just wait until you have a big problem with the opposite sex. Then maybe you'll be more understanding."

"Maybe so," Megan said, pretending Cynthia's comment didn't hurt. She had no problems with the opposite sex, that was true. But she wished she did. She wished she had some romance in her life. She

3

was sure that Cynthia thought photography and writing for the newspaper and school satisfied all of Megan's needs. And usually they did, but sometimes . . .

Megan closed her eyes and the lunchroom drifted away. In its place came the dream she'd had about Cynthia the night before. She'd forgotten it until now. There was a sterile box, white, all white. And the smell of disinfectant, alcohol, and Cynthia's perfume. Cinnabar, that deep, red, exotic smell of Turkish harems and fall flowers. But mixed with the scent that matched Cynthia's personality so well was the smell of fear. An image appeared. Cynthia pale, almost as white as the sheets, the sheets in a hospital bed. She was curled up, her blond hair fanned over a pillow, so thin, so weak . . .

"Megan, for God's sake, what's wrong? Let go of my arm. You're hurting me."

Megan came back to the lunchroom, with its smells of burritos and refried beans, today's lunch. She shook her head to clear it of the frightening scene.

"What happened, Megan?" Cynthia questioned. "You seemed far away from here. You aren't getting sick, are you?"

"Of course not, but, Cynthia, I haven't been sleeping well lately—ever since school started—and I've had the strangest dreams. I was remembering the one I had last night. You were in this one. You were in a hospital and you were afraid."

"Good grief, Megan. Being a senior is tough, but we've made it this far. Hang on. Look at me. Do I look sick? No, I'm fine. Mad at Derrick. Mad at Gus, too. But I'm not sick. I haven't even had a cold for a year. I don't have time. I've got to go home and sew again tonight or I'm never going to get my dress finished for Homecoming.''

"You and Gus will get back together again, Cynthia. Don't worry." Megan played with her sandwich. All appetite for food was gone. "I know you will. You can tell Derrick that."

"I guess we will. We've fought before and made up. But he's the one who's going to have to apologize this time." Cynthia scraped the plastic bowl that had held her cottage cheese.

"Want some of my lunch?" Megan offered.

"No thanks. I'd like to fit into the dress when I do get it finished. Don't tell me you've lost your appetite. You must be the one who's sick." Cynthia laughed.

Megan tried to laugh, too, but the images that had filled her head lingered. She nibbled at a potato chip and let the salty crunch fill her mouth. She let the smell of cake take the place of antiseptic and nibbled a corner of her dessert.

Then she felt someone's eyes on her. Glancing up, she met the stare of Derrick Ames. He was three tables away, but he might as well have been face to face with her. There was something Megan hadn't told Cynthia, and she didn't know why, since they had always shared everything—sometimes Derrick scared her too. She'd tried to laugh it off, put it down to her active writer's imagination. But there was something strange about him, some weird energy that seemed to surround him. Sometimes when she stood next to him, it seemed so real she felt she could reach out and touch it—if you could touch energy. Sometimes it attracted Megan to him, as if he were an Adonis, every woman's dream of the perfect male. She wanted to follow him around, be with him all the time. Other times it repelled her, and she wanted to run just as Cynthia had earlier.

Right now there was a different look in Derrick's eyes that chilled Megan all the way through. She shivered. Gathering her lunch, she stuffed it quickly back into the paper bag. Maybe she was picking up on Cynthia's fear. She did that sometimes, felt what someone near her was feeling. But she couldn't stay in the lunchroom one more minute with Derrick staring at her like he was.

"Let's get out of here, Cynthia. I need to go outside in the sunshine. I'm cold. I guess I don't feel so good after all."

# Chapter 2

Megan didn't see Derrick again until after school at Photography Club. And then he seemed perfectly normal—normal for Derrick. He didn't seem to have any kind of energy surrounding him at all, but was slumped in a chair ignoring everyone.

"Do you want to stand up, Megan, or sit at the table with the slide projector?"

Robert Brody was helping Megan set up. Each week a different member would present photographs for entertainment and criticism. Megan was giving her slide show from her trip to India with her parents.

"I'll sit and do very little talking. I'm trying to learn to let my pictures speak for themselves." Megan smiled at Robert.

"I refuse to comment on your ability to refrain from talking," Robert said, smiling back.

"Okay, okay, I know I like to talk." Megan took the teasing well. "But just you wait and see."

"Ready, Megan?" asked Mrs. Kloverstrom, the Photo Club's sponsor.

Megan nodded, and Robert killed the lights. She clicked on her first slide. It was a close-up of a cobra rising sensuously from a basket—everyone's clichéd image of India. Then she moved to a close-up of the old snake charmer's face before throwing on her title slide, "India, Old and New."

Soon she was halfway through her show, keeping quiet, as was her resolution. She had arranged the slides so a modern scene was followed by one that could have been centuries old.

"This is one of my best photos." Megan flashed a group of gypsy women on the screen. They were clad in red cotton saris and carried brass water jugs on their heads.

Suddenly she shivered, despite her resolution to forget. The face of one of the gypsy women reminded her. She could still feel the woman's grip on her hand, see the look in her eyes.

"I tell your fortune," the woman had said, holding out her hand for money.

Megan hadn't wanted her fortune told, but the group had urged her to do so. When she had handed over her dollar, though, the gypsy woman had backed away. There had been fear in her eyes. Megan had seen the fear and felt the woman's reluctance to tell her fortune. She'd always wonder if the gypsy had seen the accident that was played out later. She shook her head to keep the awful memory of the plane crash from returning now.

"Megan, are you all right?" Robert was sitting beside her. His hand was on her arm.

"Oh, sure. Sorry." She flicked to the next slide, close-ups of the women adorned with earrings, nose rings, and necklaces. "At first the women said we couldn't take their pictures. They were afraid the camera would rob them of their souls."

"How funny," Candy Gilford said. "How did you convince them differently?"

"Our guide asked if money would help." Megan laughed. "They decided it would."

"So they were willing to sell their souls for a shilling?" Robert quipped. "Not a very strong belief, if you ask me."

"A number of cultures do feel strongly about cameras," said Mrs. Kloverstrom. "I almost had my camera taken in Morocco. And in a Masai village in Kenya, we were requested to take no photographs. Some people do think the image the camera makes steals from their souls."

"I'll bet a lot just want to get paid." Robert helped Megan change carousels.

"I never charge for photos." Bunny Browne giggled, posing seductively. "Maybe I should start saying, 'Three dollars for a piece of my soul.' "

"Wow, Bunny, you left yourself wide open with that remark." Robert laughed.

Megan took a deep breath and focused on where she was. She was safe. The accident the gypsy had seen in Megan's future was over. Think about Bunny, she told herself as she flicked more pictures on the screen. Dumb Bunny had lived up to her name again. But Megan really wanted to go home. Maybe she was getting the flu.

"Slow down, Megan," said Mrs. Kloverstrom. "Especially if you want us to help you choose photos for the competition."

Megan slowed deliberately but said nothing else until the show was over and three of her photos were selected as best.

"Good show, Megan." Robert boxed up Megan's slides. "I envy your getting to travel so much."

"Your pictures of Colorado are outstanding,

Robert. A photographer doesn't have to go far from home."

"Thanks, Megan. I keep reminding myself of that, but I do want to travel someday. Maybe be a correspondent for some newspaper or magazine. Want a ride?" Robert offered as they left the empty school building and headed for the parking lot.

"No. Derrick said he'd drop me off. Thanks." The strange feeling Megan had about Derrick at lunch was gone. She knew she must have picked up on Cynthia's dislike for Derrick.

Derrick walked on the other side of Megan. He hadn't said a word the whole meeting or during refreshment time, except for the offer of a ride. He didn't have to say much, though, as far as Megan was concerned. His photos spoke for him. While Megan considered herself and Robert good photographers, Derrick was exceptional. His work was already professional quality. Often when Megan got an excellent picture, she knew it was an accident. She figured from what she had seen so far Derrick did nothing by accident.

Each year Boulder High's Photography Club kicked off the year with a contest. Arriving on the scene in September, Derrick had walked away with first place. Megan came in second, but when she'd seen Derrick's entries, she couldn't complain. One was of an incredibly attractive girl—from his last school, he'd said. His art had enhanced her beauty. Two were ordinary neighborhood scenes made extraordinary by Derrick's eye and camera angle. The fourth was a color photo of clouds. Megan had felt she could reach out and touch their softened texture.

"Do you two want to go to Denver some

Saturday soon?'' Robert asked, closing the passenger door on Derrick's van and leaning on the open window. ''We can photograph some industrial sights for the black-and-white category. I'll drive.''

''Good idea,'' Megan answered for herself and Derrick. She hoped that if she hung around Derrick, she could learn from him. And he'd already mentioned he wanted some new photos for the art museum's upcoming contest. Robert stepped back, smiled, and waved when Megan answered.

Pulling out of the school parking lot, Derrick swerved his old Ford van to miss a pothole. He was draped over the steering wheel like a question mark, surveying the road and manhandling the van. Megan hadn't driven it, but she guessed it took the skill and manpower of its owner to nurse it along, not to mention his mechanical genius to keep it running.

When Derrick had relaxed a bit and headed for their subdivision, Megan teased him. ''Wow, you're really talkative today, Derrick. Asking me if I wanted a ride home took three words.''

Derrick grinned in his funny way, raising the corners of his lips about an eighth of an inch. ''Good show.''

''Thanks. I think I'll enlarge that picture of us on elephants crossing the river in Tiger Tops. The fog makes the picture mysterious.'' Megan thought out loud, knowing Derrick probably wouldn't answer. Being with Derrick wasn't like being with Cynthia, or even Robert; she and Derrick weren't surrounded by a comfortable silence. So she chattered, a habit she disliked in others. She wanted to ask him about Cynthia, but she didn't have the nerve.

He seemed terribly absentminded, in the fashion of real genius. Like now. Even with her talking, it was obvious his mind was a million miles away. He was probably thinking about a photo he wanted to take. Sometimes Megan thought the word *obsessed* would be a good tag for Derrick. It had taken very little time around him to realize that his work obsessed him. He had his own darkroom and said he spent a lot of time there.

"Isn't Bunny Browne the dumbest blond you ever knew?" Megan attempted to lure Derrick into a frivolous conversation. She'd tried it before, just to see if she could. "She's that cliché personified."

No luck. The funny smile again. No comment.

"Makes me glad I got brains instead of beauty." Megan wasn't fishing for a compliment. She knew she wasn't beautiful. Only her dark red hair saved her from being a real disaster. Her figure was what some would call pleasingly plump, and she didn't care. She had no desire to become prom queen or win a beauty contest. She had developed her artistic talents instead. She also knew that Derrick wouldn't lie and tell her she was attractive to make her feel better. She knew him that well. She sighed. Maybe he picked up on her feelings.

"I like you, Megan." Derrick stopped the van at her house.

"Wow! The famous photographer Derrick Ames likes me! Wow!" Megan laughed as she lifted the two boxes of slides and climbed off the high seat onto the sidewalk. "Thanks for the ride, Derrick."

"Thanks for being such an inspiration," Derrick said in response.

"I've inspired you?" Megan asked. "To do what?"

"You've reminded me of how talented I really

12

am." Derrick grinned and pulled away from the curb.

Megan watched him leave, feeling again the magnetic pull Derrick had on her. He was talented, and his pointing it out, even in teasing, didn't bother her at all. She grinned and shook her head. Derrick was something else. She had mixed emotions about him sometimes, but she was glad he had come to Boulder High. He was a fascinating person.

Megan turned the front doorknob. Locked. Even though she was late getting home, neither her mom nor her dad was there. She could get some homework done. Quickly she fished her key from her purse and let herself in. As soon as she stepped inside, however, she felt a dizziness and a fatigue overtake her. Maybe she'd been more nervous about showing her slides than she'd realized. Or her restless nights were catching up with her. She decided to take a quick nap and do homework after dinner.

Her legs turned to jelly halfway up the stairs. It was all she could do to reach her bed. What was the matter with her? She felt as if she had no control of her body at all. Losing sleep shouldn't make her feel this awful. If she could just sleep without dreaming for a night or two, even an hour or two, she knew she'd feel better.

Collapsing on her peach-flowered spread, she hugged her stuffed killer whale, the worn toy she'd had since a childhood visit to Sea World. Almost immediately she was asleep.

She smelled the smoke then. But she couldn't move. The fire surged toward her. She tugged and pulled, but she couldn't get away. There was no

13

escaping it. Clouds of smoke surrounded her. Hungry flames snapped and crackled. She twisted her wrists until they were filled with pain. She screamed and screamed, "I must get out. I must!"

# Chapter 3

"Megan, wake up!" Someone shook Megan. She grabbed the arm. "Megan, you're dreaming. Wake up." It was her father.

"Oh, Dad." Megan tried to shake off the dream. It was so real. She still felt the heat of the flames coming toward her.

"Want to tell me about it?" Mr. Davidson sat on the bed beside Megan.

Megan pulled herself to a sitting position. She felt worse than before she lay down, and she hadn't slept long. "Do you ever think about the plane wreck, Dad?" Megan asked.

"In India?" It seemed to take her dad a minute to realize what Megan was talking about. "Was that what you were dreaming about? We all got out okay, honey. Why would you continue to worry about it?"

"I—I don't know. I thought I was trapped. The flames were coming closer. I was so hot and there was smoke . . ." Megan's voice trailed off.

"Megan." Mr. Davidson ran his hand over Megan's hair and took her hand. "Megan, honey, the plane didn't catch on fire. Remember everyone saying what a blessing it was that it didn't?"

"It must have." Megan rubbed her eyes. "I was trapped and so scared." She started to cry softly.

Mr. Davidson put his palm on Megan's forehead.

"I'm not sick. I was—I was dreaming." Should she tell her dad about dreaming every time she fell asleep lately? But what could he do? Send her to a doctor, or worse, a psychiatrist? Give her a lecture about stress, or even suggest she cut down on her activities? She didn't want that. And she didn't want to worry him or her mother. "It was just a dream," she said, getting to her feet.

"Hey, come help me finish dinner. Maybe you're hungry."

"I'm always hungry, Dad. You know that. I take after you. Mom home?"

"Any minute. Come on. She left a roast in the Crockpot. We just need to make a salad and nuke some vegetables."

Mrs. Davidson burst into the kitchen just as they were dishing up dinner. She sighed, kicked off her shoes, and poured herself a cup of coffee.

"Tough day?" Megan asked.

Even tired, her mother was gorgeous. Her outfit was hardly wrinkled, her makeup and hair perfect. She was such a contrast to Megan and her father. Megan had pulled on jeans and Mr. Davidson was in rumpled corduroys.

A model for products aimed at adults, Mrs. Davidson traveled the metro area wearing new fashions and furs, posing in kitchens, country-club settings, on the golf course, or at some glamorous job setting. Quite often she showed up on television, talking about the car of the future or the perfume that set middle-aged men's hearts pounding.

"I did three sessions. I can't believe I'm so crazy.

But they wanted me. It's hard to say no. But, how was your photo show, Megan?"

"Lots of compliments and some ideas for enlargements. I guess I'll enter the art museum's show after all."

"Great. Hey, thanks for finishing dinner." Mom sat at the table and let Megan wait on her. "I'll do dishes. And then soak my feet. I'm exhausted. I may stay home tomorrow."

"That's what you get for being so beautiful and talented." Mr. Davidson smiled at his wife.

"Look, it takes no talent to stand in front of a camera all day. Just strength. Lots of it." Mrs. Davidson helped herself to salad and vegetables and a small portion of meat.

Megan laughed. Her mother would probably do three more jobs tomorrow. She was some kind of superwoman. "Maybe you're really tired because you're losing your soul." Megan reminded her mother about the gypsy's belief about their cameras. Since she couldn't forget about the episode, she might as well talk about it. Sometimes that helped.

"No, your mother's getting paid, remember," Megan's dad said.

They laughed and talked, and Megan pushed her dreams, more recently becoming nightmares, aside. She'd had dreams before where she kept trying to get to school. Or she was entering a contest and kept searching for a photo she'd lost. Your usual stress dreams. She was just physically tired. She wasn't as good at working under stress as her mother. With homework, a newspaper deadline every week, photos due on the annual, she was almost too busy. She had a right to be tired.

Megan helped her mom with dishes so they could

both get out of the kitchen in a hurry. "Do you ever think of the plane crash, Mom?"

As her father had done, Megan's mother looked at Megan for a minute, her face blank. "Oh, no, Megan. I had to remember what you were talking about. Now that my arm has healed, it's history. You aren't worried about it, are you? Goodness, no reason for that."

Mrs. Davidson had broken her arm when their twin-engine Otter had crashed, returning from their hop to Tiger Tops in Nepal. Megan and her dad had escaped with only bruises. But even as Megan talked to her mother, she wondered why her mother and father had been able to forget the event that was starting to haunt her. Why couldn't she forget it?

As if her mother had read her mind, she said, "Sometimes, when something bad happens, Megan, we push it away and refuse to deal with it. Maybe you didn't deal with the crash at the time, and you have to think about it now."

"You may be right, Mom. I've been dreaming about it. It happened so fast, I don't even remember being scared. But I feel scared now. Isn't that strange?"

"Sounds as if you have a bad attack of what-might-have-happened. Brought back by looking at your slides, I'd bet. We survived. Think that over and let it go." Megan's mom hugged her close for a minute. Megan hugged back, grateful for parents who didn't laugh at her fears.

"You're pretty smart—for a mother," Megan said teasingly, and joined her mother's soft laughter.

She stopped to kiss her dad when dishes were done.

"Want to watch TV?" he asked. "There's a dance concert on Channel 6."

"No, I have to study, and I want to go to bed early. Newspaper staff meeting in the morning, remember?" Megan hurried up the stairs.

Before she started her chemistry problems, she reached for the phone.

"Don't do that," Cynthia said.

"Do what?"

"Answer the phone before it rings. It gives me the creeps."

Megan hadn't realized she'd answered before the phone rang. "Oh, it was good timing, Cynthia. I was just going to call you before I got involved with chemistry. I'm afraid the only chemistry I'm really interested in is the reaction of chemicals on film."

"How about male and female? Gus just called me. He's coming over to take me for a Coke. Sounds serious." Cynthia laughed.

"What did I tell you? He's been planning an apology all day. Don't be too hard on him."

"I will at first, but I'll give in. Now I really can tell Derrick I can't go with him. Everyone knows the Homecoming Queen goes with the football captain. Did Robert ask to take you to the dance at the Photo Club meeting today?"

"No. What makes you think he will? We'll both take pictures at the game and the dance. He wouldn't even consider that either of us needs a date."

"I think he likes you, Megan, more than you realize. Maybe even more than he realizes. It's obvious."

"Sure he likes me. We're good friends." Megan was used to Cynthia's being an incurable romantic.

"Okay, maybe Derrick will ask you when I turn him down."

"He'll be taking pictures too." Megan reminded her.

"Oh, you. Sometimes I think you're already married to that camera. There is more to life, Megan."

"Yeah, homework. Go get ready to see Gus, Cynthia. I'm going to be up all night as it is." Megan laughed at Cynthia and hung up. She had known that Cynthia and Gus would get back together.

She stopped laughing immediately. She would like a date to the dance, she realized. Even if she was going to be working, taking photos. You're feeling sorry for yourself, she told herself. She hated it when that happened. Put all Cynthia's romantic ideas away immediately, she ordered. And study. She was behind in everything. Maybe she *would* study all night instead of going to bed early. Or she'd keep at it until she was too tired to dream.

A realization worse than no date for the dance came into her mind. It expanded and pushed out all other thoughts. The dreams. Suddenly the idea of going to sleep had become frightening.

# Chapter 4

Derrick had made a habit of picking up Megan on Tuesday mornings. She'd slept heavily and gotten up late, so there was no time for breakfast. She stood on the curb, waiting, sipping a cup of Red Zinger herb tea. She had tucked an orange into her shoulder bag for peeling while they tackled the Friday edition. Her sleep had been without dreams, so she felt much better.

Derrick screeched to a stop long enough for Megan to pull herself into the passenger seat. He didn't speak, his pause for her to jump aboard his only acknowledgment that she existed. Megan made no attempt at small talk. She would have liked to ask Derrick about his inviting Cynthia to the Homecoming Dance. She knew, though, he'd never answer any questions about his personal life—if he had any personal life—so she kept quiet. Derrick looked especially tired, as if he'd been up all night.

The meeting started off quietly, but Robert, editor of *The Owl,* was a morning person. He was skilled at waking up his staff and getting them excited about the next week's paper. He talked about pieces written for Friday, nagged those behind on deadlines, and handed out assignments for the next edition.

"Derrick, will you photograph the Homecoming ceremonies at the game? Let's do a photo piece on the queen and her attendants. The annual will want copies, don't forget."

Bunny Browne was waking up. Megan marveled that she even attempted the newspaper work, but then journalism class was easier than chemistry or algebra.

"Shoot me first, Derrickie-poo." Bunny ran her hands through Derrick's kinky hair. He flushed slightly but gave Bunny a withering look, almost as if he hated her. Megan hid a smile. Bunny was too insensitive to realize Derrick's reaction.

Derrick didn't say much aloud, but his expressive gray eyes revealed his thoughts and feelings. Megan figured she was the only one who noticed. Certainly not Bunny, Homecoming Attendant, thinking about her picture in the paper again or the annual. Bunny never considered that any guy might dislike her.

Bunny went on. "We're practicing in the gym with our dresses today at noon. I can pose in the courtyard, Derrick."

Robert left it to Derrick to make appointments with those he wanted to photograph. "Megan, you and I can shoot the football game. Try for some really great action shots."

Megan nodded, pleased. She loved running up and down the field, capturing the action. She would have hated Derrick's "beauty" assignments.

"Now, the week after Homecoming is always a letdown," Robert continued. "What can we do to jazz it up?"

"Why don't we let Megan do an article on India and use some of her pictures?" David Mews said.

"No one is interested in travel articles." Megan wanted to forget India. "We should stick to local news."

"How about an article about superstitions in various cultures. You know, the photo-soul idea and others like that?" David always had good ideas. He would brainstorm until one hit the fancy of the group.

"We can combine some local stuff with Halloween, then photograph Halloween on the mall for a follow-up issue." David got excited.

"That's not a bad idea, David." Robert was thinking out loud. "How about combining it with local people's superstitions? We can interview the mayor, teachers, local celebrities about their favorite superstitions."

"Boulder is not without some weird people and ideas," said Miss Hubbard, laughing. "Especially when you've moved here from Straight-City USA." Miss Hubbard had moved to Boulder from the midwest. She'd been carefully conservative herself until the staff managed to loosen her up a little last year. But only a little. Fortunately, she usually went along with staff ideas.

"I'll say. What other small city has a witch's shop across from the university?" David laughed.

"And psychics listed in the phone book?" Robert stood up and paced the floor. "I think we're onto a good story now."

"I'll interview the witch at the Pentagram. I understand she's a white witch, and friendly," Naomi Kelly volunteered.

"I'd like my fortune told." Bunny giggled.

"Pardon me for saying so, Bunny," Robert said, "but I think your fortunes are slightly predictable. I'd like Megan to visit the psychic and write that story."

"No way." Megan was surprised by her reaction. She almost got to her feet as a wave of fear and stubbornness washed over her. "I mean, that's not my type of story, Robert. Let someone else do it."

Megan was aware of some people having psychic powers. In fact, she had done some reading when she began thinking that the pictures that occasionally flashed into her mind might be some type of psychic phenomena. But the idea frightened her.

All this dreaming she was doing since school started scared her. The pictures were so real, and intense, as if they were really happening to her. She was used to little things, like knowing Cynthia was going to call. Knowing what her mom and dad were thinking had always seemed normal. Quite often she knew way in advance what she was getting for Christmas and birthdays, but it never spoiled the gifts. She figured she was just very sensitive to people close to her. She could easily pick up on their feelings.

Megan's attention came back to the staff meeting. Without wanting to, she turned to find Derrick staring at her. He grinned, but she didn't smile back. She looked away quickly, feeling foolish. Had *he* picked up on *her* fear of this psychic business? She realized he was in one of his strange moods. His eyes flirted and teased. She surely hoped he wasn't considering inviting her to the dance if Cynthia said no, which she would do now. Megan could be Derrick's friend, but no way could she think of him as a date.

"I think that kind of thing is hokey." Jim Rawlings was the paper's skeptic.

It seemed that while Megan's mind had drifted, everyone had refused the assignment of interviewing the psychic.

"You have more nerve than any of us, Megan," said Naomi. "I still think you should do it. If you get a good fortune, then I'll go."

"Me too," Bunny added, her arm around Jim now. "I don't think I'm *that* predictable. Sometimes I have very deep thoughts that no one could guess."

Bunny didn't care if everyone laughed at her pouting face. Just so she got their attention.

"I'm sorry," Megan said firmly. "I have more than I can get done now. I can't go."

Robert looked at Megan, but she held her ground. She didn't say no to his assignments often.

"Okay, I'll do it," he said. "I'm not sure I believe in this stuff, either, but maybe I'll learn something."

Megan turned her attention back to peeling her orange as the meeting broke up. She concentrated on chewing the sweet slices. She knew everyone had left the room but Robert. She knew he stood staring at her. She could feel his mind searching hers. She focused on nothing except the orange.

"Are you sure you're all right, Megan?" he said finally. "You didn't seem yourself yesterday. And today you've decided to argue with your boss." He switched from a serious tone to teasing.

She didn't look at him, and she ignored his teasing. "Of course. I'm just busy, that's all. I shouldn't have to take every assignment you hand out."

She hadn't meant to speak so sharply. She felt his

puzzled thoughts and his hurt as he left the room. He did like her. Now that Cynthia had called her attention to it, Megan picked up on it immediately. He thought of her as more than just a reporter or a photographer. More than just a business partner. Tears sprang to her eyes. You dumb bunny, she thought as she brushed them aside. Why didn't you tell Robert that the idea of going to a psychic was frightening? He might not understand that either, but he wouldn't take it personally. She didn't have to hurt his feelings because of her fears. Suddenly she wanted badly for Robert to invite her to the dance. She wanted more time to explore these new feelings. Or were they feelings that had been there for a long time and that she was just now acknowledging?

The orange tasted flat, like old cardboard. She shivered, cold all over. Getting up, she poured a cup of coffee from the newspaper office's pot. She warmed her hands on the cup and sniffed the toasty aroma. She'd lived seventeen years without screwing up her life badly. Was she going to start now? There wasn't any reason for her to be afraid of Robert's liking her. And now she knew he did. She'd think about that all day. Robert was certainly safer subject matter than all that hokey psychic stuff.

A better mood came over her, and she felt she could head for her first class.

# Chapter 5

Although Megan thought about Robert, she ignored him and everyone else for a couple of days. She concentrated on her studies, on zipping through her classes. That always brought her back to real life. The idea of graduating in May was starting to sink in. It didn't seem possible, but if she didn't keep up her grades, it wouldn't *be* possible.

Robert found her in the newspaper office, typing, on Thursday morning. He said nothing about her refusing to write the article for the paper. He was all business.

"Megan, have you seen Derrick? He wasn't in school yesterday, and I can't find him this morning either. He's not in first period. He was supposed to have some pictures of Cynthia and her attendants for Naomi's article on Homecoming. I can't go to press without them."

"He took the pictures last night. Cynthia told me."

Cynthia had also told Megan she'd hated every minute of posing for Derrick. She'd let him know right off that she'd made up with Gus and was going to the dance with him. She said Derrick didn't seem angry, but he kept smiling at her the whole time he took the photos for the paper. It gave her the creeps.

"Derrick is always on time with his photos. He's my most dependable photographer." Robert paced the floor.

"Maybe he's at home working on them," Megan suggested. "I'll bet he'll deliver by noon."

"If he doesn't, will you cut out of lunch early and go with me to his house? I called there and got no answer."

"He's probably in his darkroom. I think he lives there."

By noon there was still no Derrick and no photos. Megan and Robert left before the lunch hour was over, but she knew she'd still be late for history class. Megan didn't mind. Living today was more interesting than studying the past. Especially being with Robert. He didn't seem angry at her and had probably forgotten her sharpness. In case he hadn't, she apologized.

"Robert, I'm sorry about being so negative the other morning about the psychic. It's just a hang-up that I have about that kind of thing."

"No problem. I interviewed her and she seemed like a perfectly normal person."

Megan laughed. "She didn't tell you a mysterious redheaded woman might enter your life?" She dared to flirt.

"No, but sounds like a good idea. Will you go to the Homecoming Dance with me, Megan? We'll need to take pictures, but we might sneak in a dance or two."

"All play and no work." Megan teased to hide her excitement.

"Makes for no newspaper and the end of our reputation for the best school paper west of the Mississippi. I'll risk it." Robert laughed.

"Me too. I'd love to go."

Robert's Camaro was a welcome change from Derrick's van. It was metallic blue and hummed like the well-cared-for machine that it was. Robert had bought the car himself and fixed it up. He smiled at Megan. She felt a slight stirring in the pit of her stomach that hadn't been there before when she looked at him.

At the beginning of the school year Derrick had moved into a rambling, two-story Spanish-style house two blocks from Megan's. It spoke of money with its cultivated yard and patio. There was a wrought-iron sculpture on the patio area, abstract, expensive, strange-looking.

"Some people's idea of art is far from mine," Robert joked.

"Derrick's mother's, to be exact. There are more of the same style inside. Some are marble." Megan had only been inside Derrick's house once, when the neighbors had surprised the Ameses with a welcoming party. During that visit Derrick had shown Megan the darkroom he'd built in his bedroom. It was the best one Megan had ever been in. Even so, the house was a cold, unwelcoming place.

Mrs. Ames answered the door. She was a heavyset woman with pampered hands and stylish hair, overdressed for a Thursday afternoon. Megan thought she had probably been beautiful once, but she looked used-up now.

"Your phone may be out of order, Mrs. Ames,"

Robert said. "I tried to call several times. Is Derrick home?"

"I was playing bridge. Just got home. Derrick has a cold, and I made him stay home." Mrs. Ames smiled. Megan found her sticky-sweet personality hard to take. She was divorced, and she and Derrick lived alone. And the rumor around the development was that she had a drinking problem. Megan suspected that Mrs. Ames spoiled Derrick terribly, and she also seemed to treat him like a baby. "You know his health is delicate." She didn't invite Megan and Robert in. They stood awkwardly on the porch.

Robert was getting impatient. "He has some pictures we need for the newspaper, Mrs. Ames. Would you call him?"

"He doesn't like to be disturbed when he's in his darkroom. He spends far too much time in there."

"Can we go up to his room?" Megan suggested.

"Oh no. I'll go up there. He might need something by now anyway." Mrs. Ames motioned for Robert and Megan to come in and headed upstairs—somewhat reluctantly, it seemed to Megan. In fact, she detected a hint of fear in Mrs. Ames's voice and manner. Was Derrick nasty when his mother disturbed him?

As they waited Megan began to feel a funny itching around her wrists. She rubbed them and the itch turned to pain. She shook both hands to get rid of the sensation.

"I'm glad I'm not an only child," Robert said, distracting Megan.

"You've forgotten that I am. But my parents don't treat me like that, thank goodness. Maybe that's why Derrick is so quiet. There's no one at home that he wants to talk to.''

''Where's his father?''

''I don't think anyone knows. I can see why he left his wife though,'' Megan whispered, stifling a giggle.

''Naughty, naughty.'' Robert fingered a wrought-iron sculpture that moved slowly when touched. It balanced on a piece of marble and stainless steel.

Mrs. Ames cleared her throat as if to say Robert shouldn't touch things. ''Derrick is busy. He handed me this packet through the door.''

Robert took the manila envelope and shuffled through the pictures. ''Thanks, Mrs. Ames. This is what I need.''

Megan led the way out of the house, with its cloying atmosphere. There was a look in Mrs. Ames's eyes that Megan didn't like. She couldn't put a label on it, but she made some connection to her wrists itching again. The sensation stopped the minute she got back in Robert's car.

''Did you get a creepy feeling, being in there?'' Megan asked Robert.

''Just that I wouldn't want to live there. Seemed like an unpopular museum. I don't blame Derrick for hiding out in his darkroom.''

''This may sound crazy, but I got the idea that Mrs. Ames was afraid of something, maybe even Derrick.''

''Yes, that's crazy, Megan. She was probably just a little tipsy.'' Robert laughed.

Megan shrugged off the idea and shuffled through the pictures as Robert headed for school. Cynthia, Bunny, Roxie MacNeil, Marva James, Candy Gilford, and Lora Santana. Pasteboard smiles on pasteboard girls. Except for Cynthia, none of the beauties had much going for her except looks. Was it true that when you were physically beautiful, you didn't have to work so hard to cultivate talent or inner beauty? Or was that a cliché? Five of these six girls just happened to be among those who didn't bother to cultivate anything else.

Actually, Lora Santana loved horses and was a good rider. She'd been Stock Show Queen last year. Roxie and Bunny worked on the paper, but they confined their news to lightweight subject matter. Roxie was good at layout and collecting ads. Merchants dazzled by her looks probably bought ads to see her smile.

Megan scolded herself. She was being catty, and maybe even a bit jealous of such an array of glamour. Derrick had done his job well. They all looked relaxed, beautiful, and were caught in a good light, one that flattered their features. If Derrick ever wanted to do fashion photography, he'd be successful.

"Thanks, Megan. For some reason I didn't want to go out there alone. I hope you won't get any flak for being late to your history class." Robert parked his car in the school lot and they scrambled out.

It was worth it, Megan thought. She was excited about the weekend now. She was really looking forward to Homecoming.

# Chapter 6

An incredible amount of exhilaration filled Megan as she dressed for the Homecoming Dance. This was silly, she thought. She was only going out with Robert, her good friend. They'd spend most of the evening taking photos.

"I'm so glad you decided to go, Megan," her mother said. "I've had my eye on this dress for weeks. I saw it first in a show at May D & F. And I guess I'd better confess." Megan's mom giggled, actually giggled. Megan looked at her with surprise. "I put it on layaway."

"Mom, you didn't." Megan laughed and looked at herself in the full-length mirror in her mother's room. "What if I wasn't invited to any dances this year?"

"Oh, I knew you would be."

The dress was a dusty pink, surprisingly flattering despite Megan's red hair. One of Megan's shoulders was left bare and on the other was a huge pink rose made of layers and layers of chiffon. It seemed to float over her shoulder when she twirled. She wore soft maroon slippers that had tiny heels. Her long, thick hair was clean and shiny and swirled around her shoulders. Pink-and-maroon earrings dangled from her ears, but they were the only jewelry she wore. Having a mother who was a model had taught her that simple styles were really more eye-catching than lots of ruffles and baubles. For her, anyway. As a rule, Megan didn't wear makeup, but tonight her mother had skillfully made up Megan's face with just a touch of foundation, eye shadow, and mascara. Megan was amazed at the difference it made in her looks. Huge green eyes sparkled, almost laughing back at her from the mirror.

When she floated into the living room, where Robert was visiting with her father, she had to hold back her laughter. Robert was momentarily speechless, but Megan could feel his surprise and admiration. He didn't expect her to wear her usual braid and jeans, did he? Too bad she had to swing the heavy camera case over her shoulder instead of carrying a simple clutch purse.

Robert grabbed the bag from her. "I may forget we're there on business," he whispered as they left the Davidson house. "You look . . ." Robert searched for the right word.

Megan had to laugh then. "Gorgeous, beautiful, lovely—any of those will do."

"All of those." Robert laughed, too, and they both relaxed. "Have I ever seen you in a dress?"

"I should hope so. But maybe not. Hey, this is an occasion."

The gym was decorated in harvest style, with pumpkins, dried cornstalks, and big bales of hay to sit on or to use for tables. Everyone spoke to Robert and Megan, and Megan gathered many compliments, even from guys. Suddenly she felt popular and pleased with herself. Maybe she should give more time to her appearance, care more how she looked. She knew she had lots of friends, but she'd usually stayed in the background of school life, taking pictures, writing stories, observing what other people did.

Almost immediately Megan noticed Derrick snapping pictures all over the gym. He had two cameras slung around his neck and looked very official. He hadn't even bothered to dress up, but wore khaki fatigues as usual. It was as if he were saying, I am here only to record this frivolity.

Robert found them a table and waved at Gus and Cynthia to join them. Cynthia sat beside Megan and whispered, "That Derrick is driving me crazy, Megan. Every time I turn around, he snaps my picture."

"Take it as a compliment, Cynthia. You look lovely."

Cynthia wore the shimmering gown she'd created for the Homecoming ceremonies and the dance. It was hard to believe she'd made it herself instead of discovering it in one of Denver's fancy boutiques. There were tiny gold beads all over the cream chiffon that caught and reflected the light. A peach-colored shawl covered her shoulders, and at her waist was a spray of peach-colored roses tied with a brown ribbon. Her white-blond hair was piled high, and here and there tendrils escaped in a sexy, teasing fashion.

"So do you, Megan." Cynthia took a good look at Megan for the first time. "That dress is lovely. Let me guess. Your mom picked it out."

"You don't think I have good taste?" Megan teased.

"I think you have excellent taste." She leaned

close and whispered. "In guys. I just know what kind of clothes you usually wear."

"Maybe I'll change my image, starting tonight." Megan grinned, and Cynthia squeezed her arm.

While they whispered, Derrick kneeled in front of Cynthia and snapped her picture. The flash startled Megan, and she could see that Derrick was being annoying. No one liked lights flashing in her eyes every few minutes. Megan also picked up on the anger building in Cynthia.

"It's starting to be an invasion of privacy," Cynthia complained. "I'm sure he has all the photos he needs for the paper or the annual."

"Do you want me to have Robert speak to him?" Megan asked. Maybe that would be a good way to approach Derrick, she thought. Then it wouldn't seem to come as a direct complaint from Cynthia. She had a right to be frustrated with Derrick, though. Megan wondered if this was Derrick's way of getting even with Cynthia because she'd turned him down for the dance. He had to know he was bugging Cynthia, interfering with her fun.

"No, I hate to give him the satisfaction of knowing I care."

"You *are* a celebrity. Ignore him and enjoy being with Gus and knowing you look beautiful." Megan sipped the Coke Robert had brought her. He and Gus had disappeared for a few minutes, leaving the girls to chat.

"Want to dance?" Robert asked Megan when he returned. "Derrick seems to be taking enough photos for us all. I think we can relax and have a good time."

Megan stood up and took Robert's hand. "Aren't

you dancing?'' she said to Cynthia before they walked onto the floor.

"If Gus doesn't mind, we'll sit this one out. I'm a bit tired,'' Cynthia said, taking Gus's hand.

Cynthia did look tired. Even in the dim lighting, Megan could see the dark circles under her eyes. She had probably sewn for nights, and now, last night's game and tonight's celebration were taking their toll on her energy.

"I developed some of your photos from last night, Megan,'' Robert said as they moved to the beat of the slow number. "They're excellent, better than most of mine. Having you and Derrick on my staff this year has sure made the job easy.''

"Robert, Derrick has taken many more photos of Cynthia than necessary tonight. If you get a chance to do it tactfully, would you tell him you think that's enough?''

"He does get carried away with his work, doesn't he?'' Robert said. "Look at him. Two cameras.'' Robert chuckled.

They were on the other side of the gym when the number finished, so Robert suggested they dance the next. Megan didn't complain. She could dance with Robert all evening. Forget work.

So she didn't see what happened. But she knew instantly that something was wrong with Cynthia. "It's Cynthia, Robert. Something's happened.''

By then people had stopped dancing and begun to talk. "Cynthia.'' "Cynthia.'' "Cynthia.'' The name carried from person to person like an echo coming toward Megan.

Megan left Robert and pushed through the crowd. "Let me past, please! What's happened? She's my friend. Let me get to her." An aisle opened for Megan when people heard the urgency in her voice.

"Cynthia!" Megan screamed without meaning to. Beside their table Cynthia had collapsed in a pool of shimmering gold beads and cream chiffon. Gus knelt, cradling Cynthia's head in his lap.

"What happened, Gus?" Megan questioned.

"I don't know." Gus was practically in tears. "She got up. We'd started out to the dance floor. She didn't even say anything, just passed out, almost before I could catch her."

Robert reached them. "Has anyone called an ambulance? Should we take her to the hospital?"

"Let's wait a minute," Megan suggested. "Cynthia, Cynthia?" Megan tried to get her friend to gain consciousness. She frantically racked her brain trying to remember what she had learned in her first-aid class. "Move the crowd back, Robert. She needs air. Cynthia?" Megan patted Cynthia's cheeks lightly. She seemed so far away. A pinpoint of fear started to form in Megan's stomach. Cynthia was deathly pale and her skin was cold. "Call an ambulance, Robert. I can't get her to come around at all."

As Robert stood and ran for the office to phone, Megan focused on the crowd, milling around with concerned looks on their faces. Her eyes stopped on one face that held no element of concern. Derrick slouched near them, his cameras dangling, leaning on a post that was wrapped with autumn leaves. On his face was the tiny grin, his lips curled so slightly that only someone who knew him would realize he was smiling.

The fear inside Megan started to grow like the nucleus of something evil.

# Chapter 7

Megan and Robert followed the ambulance to the hospital, but for a time all they could do was sit in the waiting room and worry. Gus paced the floor, unable to sit still.

"She has to be all right, she just has to," he said.

"She will be, Gus," Megan reassured him. "I think she was exhausted from all the fuss, getting ready for the ceremonies, staying up late sewing." Megan comforted herself as well as Gus.

Mrs. Harlow sent them all home. "There's no reason for all of you to stay here, Megan," she said. "The doctor has taken some blood samples, and he wants Cynthia to stay the night and rest. She seems okay now. The doctor thinks she may have fainted from exhaustion. I told Cynthia she was working too hard." Mrs. Harlow smiled at Megan and patted her hand, but she looked tired too.

Megan and Robert were quiet on the trip across town, each thinking their own thoughts about the evening. But at Megan's door, Robert pulled Megan close.

"You're a good friend, Megan, to me and to Cynthia. Her getting sick makes me realize how much I care for you. If that had been you—"

"It wasn't, Robert." Megan cut off his worrying. "Cynthia has never been too strong. Sometimes I think she doesn't eat right, trying to stay so thin. Fortunately, I don't have that trouble." Megan's stomach fluttered at Robert's standing so close. She tried to tease to make herself relax.

"You looked great tonight, Megan." Robert laughed. "Great? Some writer I am. You looked fantastic, beautiful . . ."

"A good editor is going to cut this copy," Megan whispered.

"So I'll shut up and show you what I think."

Robert kissed her, a warm, loving kiss that did let Megan know he cared for her. She returned the kiss and for a long time they stood, Robert holding her, soothing away all the worry of the evening for both of them.

"I'll call you tomorrow. If Cynthia is still in the hospital and you want to go over, I'll come get you."

"Thanks, Robert." Megan slipped inside, wanting to keep the memory of his kiss instead of the rest of the evening.

The doctor let Cynthia go home on Sunday, since nothing showed up on the tests he'd given her. But she didn't go to school on Monday.

The school was abuzz with rumors. Megan didn't stop to listen to any of them or to correct anything people were saying. There really wasn't anything to say yet. She didn't see Robert until lunchtime, when he flopped down beside her in the lunchroom. He smiled, but he was all business, the dance and the kiss a memory.

"Will you help Bunny write the Homecoming story, Megan? I should never have given it to her,

40

but she begged. Now she's having trouble finishing it. She has the facts, but there's no life to it. You've spoiled me with your lively writing."

Helping Bunny would be a drag. It would be so much easier to write the piece herself. But Megan said yes—for Robert, not for Bunny.

"How is Cynthia today?" Robert bit into a taco and it crumbled all around him. He shook his head and gathered up the scraps onto his plate.

"I didn't get to talk to her, but her mom said the doctor thought it was stress and exhaustion. She worked hard getting ready for Homecoming."

"Yeah, she did. Bunny and Roxie and the others spent big bucks on dresses. Cynthia took it as a challenge to make hers. She has a lot of talent." Robert looked at Megan, making her feel warm all over. "So do you, Megan. We make a good news team."

Megan felt her cheeks grow hot. Don't be silly, she scolded herself. This is just Robert, your partner in gathering all the news worth reading about in Boulder High. She tried to change the subject to the Halloween issue of the newspaper.

Robert changed it back to them. "The mall celebration will be after the Friday paper is out, but will you go with me? We can get some good pictures."

"Sure, Robert," said Megan, trying to think of it as work, not a date. She didn't want to get all silly over a guy. "I'd like that."

Megan called to Bunny, who was sitting one table over, in order to cover her sudden embarrassment over Robert. "Bunny, meet me in the newspaper office after school?"

Bunny waved her yes. Megan gathered the rest of

41

her lunch quickly. "I need to stop by the library before history, Robert." She might as well study. Sitting by Robert, she was having trouble eating. Maybe she'd lose ten pounds because of her new relationship with him.

Bunny was in a strange mood when Megan met her after school. She sprawled across the newspaper desk. "I think I'm having post-Homecoming depression, Megan. Suddenly I'm tired. Tired of school, tired of the newspaper, the whole thing. I can't even get this story started. Maybe I really am dumb."

"Hey, Bunny," Megan said, trying to cheer her up, "where's your great sense of humor? You probably are tired, but we have a deadline."

"I'm tired of deadlines, too. You write the story for me, Megan, will you? I'd be eternally grateful."

Megan sighed. Bunny did look tired, and she wasn't acting like herself. "Okay, just this once. Go on home and get some sleep."

Megan shook off the heavy feeling she'd picked up from Bunny and dashed off the article. Robert would know it was hers, and he was the only one she cared about. Mrs. Hubbard was pretty lax. She left all the glory, as well as the work, to her students. She'd never realize it wasn't Bunny's story.

By Friday, when Cynthia wasn't back in school, Megan stopped by her house with a dozen copies of *The Owl*. Cynthia was propped up by several pillows in her canopy bed. She looked pale and wan. Megan felt a shiver of fear race through her at Cynthia's appearance.

"Mother insisted I have some tests, so I've been to the doctor again today. They took so much blood I'm probably anemic by now." Cynthia's nightgown was white, and with her hair the Nordic blond and her face colorless, she was almost the picture that Megan had seen in her dream.

"What did he say?" Megan took Cynthia's hand. It was cold.

"He suspects mono. Says it's hard to diagnose unless you catch it at one exact moment. Just what I need to liven up my senior year, isn't it?" Cynthia smiled.

"I still vote for your wearing yourself out before the dance, Cyn."

"I confess I did. But this bug was waiting to get me. When I got tired, my resistance was down. Phooey, I'll miss Halloween."

"Robert and I are going to take pictures on the mall."

"Hey, you sure you can mix going out with your boss and working for him?" Cynthia said, teasing.

"I'd like to try."

They looked at the newspaper. There was a huge picture story on the Homecoming ceremonies, the football game, the dance. There were photos of Cynthia on the field, individual photos of her and her attendants in the formal shots Derrick had made before the dance. Robert had included several informal photos of Cynthia at the dance before she fainted. She did look beautiful.

"Megan, thanks for coming over," Mrs. Harlow said, breaking up the gossip session. "But Cynthia needs to rest."

"I'll bring some homework next week if you aren't back, Cynthia," Megan promised as she left. She wondered if Cynthia would feel like studying, though. She couldn't help but worry about her friend.

\* \* \*

Derrick picked up Megan as usual for the next Tuesday's staff meeting. Since there was no way to tell him she didn't feel comfortable around him, she made the best of it.

"Great photo, Derrick," Robert said when Derrick opened his briefcase and pulled out his new work.

"Hey, I like it!" Candy Gilford grabbed the picture. She was draped in chiffon in front of a crystal ball. "No one would suspect it's an upside-down light globe. Your lighting makes it look real."

Derrick smiled, but Megan noticed that he looked tired. Had he stayed up all night developing photos? Senior year was going to kill them all if they weren't careful.

"I'm going to use it for the front page," Robert said. "I sure wish we had some more Halloween photos. The timing is off, with Halloween coming the day after the paper comes out."

"We can take photos early, pretending they're from the mall celebration," Derrick suggested in an unusual burst of words. "I'll pose some of the girls in costume."

"Wait till you see what my mom brought from New York." Roxie MacNeil brought out a big dress box she'd been saving for a surprise. She'd brought them to show Bunny, but now she could show them off to everyone.

Everyone gasped when she opened the box. There were two incredible fairy costumes, one gold and one white. Skimpy leotards were covered with sequins and ruffles and beads. The wings were gauze, painted with silver or gold.

"I'm going to wear the gold," Roxie said. "It'll go well with my red hair. You wear the silver one,

Bunny. I asked Mom to get it for you so we could go together. We'll go down to the mall tonight and pose for Derrick."

"Okay," Bunny said. She lacked her usual exuberance for getting her picture in the paper, but agreed, holding up the costume. "It is pretty."

"How about 'Two of Our Lovely Fairy Queens' for a caption?" Robert said, laughing, as they finished planning the issue.

"I really don't think Miss Hubbard will let you get by with that, Robert." Megan laughed too, knowing Robert was teasing. He seemed in an unusually good mood. "Even with as little supervision as she gives us, I'm sure she proofs every word before giving it to the print shop."

"Besides," Roxie grinned, taking the joke farther, "Bunny and I aren't *that* close. We're only good friends. Right, Bun?"

Derrick laughed out loud, actually laughed. Megan, sitting by him, had to move away. She was picking up that unusual energy from him, despite his tired appearance. She walked to the coffeepot and slowly poured herself a cup. Then she helped herself to a doughnut even though she didn't feel hungry. It gave her something to do, an excuse to move away from Derrick. His laughter had sent shivers down her back and goose bumps over her arms. His laughter hadn't come from humor, but from something she couldn't identify.

She stayed as far away from Derrick as possible until the meeting was over. Then she helped Robert clean up after the staff had left.

"Robert, have you noticed Derrick acting unusual?" Megan asked, boxing up the leftover

45

doughnuts so they wouldn't dry out. The staff could eat them throughout the day.

"Unusual? How? His work is terrific. That's not unusual, but he did get overly excited about it today. Said a whole sentence."

"And laughed out loud." Megan tried to laugh. "I had to move. I couldn't sit by him."

"Then I don't have to get jealous, do I?" Robert pulled her close and bounced a kiss off the end of her nose. "Too much imagination is not good for a reporter, my dear. The facts, just the facts."

"I don't know what the facts are."

# Chapter 8

Megan visited Cynthia every day the rest of the week. And every day she became aware of Cynthia's worsening condition.

On Friday, when Megan delivered *The Owl* with the Halloween photos, Cynthia had bad news. "Oh, Megan." Her fingers folded and pleated the pink-flowered sheets pulled up around her. "I have to go into the hospital tomorrow. The doctor wants more tests for—for leukemia."

"Cynthia, no, oh no." Megan knelt beside her friend's bed and took her slender hand. It was so cool and lifeless. "It can't be. You have to fight back, though, whatever it is. Promise me you'll fight. You have to get well."

"I'm just so tired. I don't have any fight left."

"Are you in pain?"

"No, I don't have any strength. It's as if something is just sapping all my energy. I can hardly stand up when I get out of bed."

Megan didn't know what to say. What could you say when your best friend was fading away before your eyes? She stood and paced the floor.

"I wish I could go to the mall with you for Halloween," Cynthia said, changing the subject.

"Will you come to the hospital first thing Sunday morning and tell me all about it?"

"I will, Cynthia. I promise. And I'll bring our pictures as soon as we get them developed."

On the way home from Cynthia's, Megan stopped at the photo shop where she got most of her developing and printing done. She ordered two poster-size enlargements of her photos of Cynthia in her Homecoming dress. She'd put them on the wall in Cynthia's room. Then she bought rolls of crepe paper and Halloween decorations at the drugstore next door. The hospital room was so sterile—so white. All she could do for Cynthia was try to keep her cheered up. They'd stop at the hospital on their way to the mall on Saturday night.

Robert thought that was a great idea. Even Derrick, who to Megan's dismay was going with them, seemed concerned about Cynthia and was willing to stop. She had thought she and Robert were going to the mall alone, but this really was a picture-taking expedition, not a date. She was glad she had called Bunny and Roxie and asked them to meet at the hospital in their fairy costumes. Cynthia would love the New York creations.

Megan wore a clown costume. She had long ago stopped trying to be glamorous for Halloween. It wasn't her style. She had a lime green acrylic wig— Afro style—that her mother had found in a shop in Denver. Painted on her face was the biggest smile she had room for. Her eyebrows arched in perpetual surprise. Her floppy suit was green with orange polka dots, and she'd painted an old pair of her dad's shoes orange with green dots. White gloves with a mass of colored pompons on the wrists completed her outfit. As she entered the hospital room she hoped the painted-on smile would hide her sadness for Cynthia.

They strung the crepe paper across the room while Cynthia and her roommate giggled. Cynthia's roommate had a broken leg and was much more energetic than Cynthia. She clapped and cheered for the unexpected celebration.

"How'd you break your leg, Geri?" Megan asked.

"In a warm-up basketball game." Geri made a face. "Now I'll miss basketball season as well as skiing."

Bunny and Roxie appeared just in time to see the last witch taped on the wall. The girls looked like twins despite their different coloring.

"Fantastic," Cynthia squealed at the sight of the fairy costumes. "I wish I had made them."

"Now for the finale. Ta-ta-ta-da!" Robert, dressed appropriately in a magician's outfit, pulled out a big bag he'd saved for last. In it was a tall, black witch's hat. He placed it on Cynthia's head. Propped up by pillows, she managed a smile. "Let's have a photo, Derrick," Robert suggested. "Not for publication," he assured Cynthia. "But for your scrapbook—the time you bewitched all the doctors at Community Hospital."

Megan posed a fairy on either side of Cynthia. First they perched beside her, then did ballet poses, holding to the railing at the head of the bed, tapping Cynthia with wands topped by gold and silver stars. Derrick, again with two cameras, snapped several photos with each to insure some good shots. Megan noticed that Bunny was quieter than usual, but she looked incredibly beautiful in the silver-and-white costume. Megan caught one glimpse of herself in a mirror and tried not to compare clowns and fairies. The world needed both, she reminded herself.

"Cynthia should get magically better." Roxie tapped Cynthia on the head with her wand. "I command it." They laughed and wished Cynthia well as they left.

"Why don't we all ride together?" Robert asked Bunny and Roxie. "Leave your car here. It will be hard enough to park one car near the mall."

Bunny and Roxie surrounded Derrick in the small backseat, amid much tickling and giggling. Derrick, in a cowboy costume, looked totally out of place and uncomfortable.

"Kiss me or I'll shoot." Roxie had stolen Derrick's gun from its holster and teased him with it.

Megan couldn't resist spying on the trio as Roxie kissed Derrick and Bunny looked on, giggling, waiting her turn.

"If we get separated, which is certainly possible in this crowd," Robert said, "meet back at the car at midnight. The crowd gets wilder after that, and surely we'll have had enough of this madness. Agreed?"

Everyone thought midnight was a good witching hour for the end of the fun, and they started off together. Boulder at Halloween was like a Mardi Gras celebration. Throngs of merrymakers flocked to the outside mall, which was closed off to traffic. There was every conceivable costume: yellow Venus pencils and a ruler, old hags and elegant movie stars, all manner of aliens and outer-space characters, three couch potatoes, California raisins, Super Priest, Miss Muffet and her spider, the president, Prince Charles and Diana, pirates, and a wonderful

Quasimodo. Soon all of them were squashed together and had to move with the crowd whether or not they wanted to.

Robert and Derrick helped Bunny and Roxie, both five foot two, onto lampposts so they could see and people could see them. Everyone in the vicinity cheered at the beauty of their costumes. The girls struck flying poses and waved their wands.

Derrick, the cowboy with cameras, took several photos of the almost-twins before crowds swept him, Megan, and Robert forward, separating them from Bunny and Roxie. At every opportunity Robert and Megan snapped pictures. But stopping to focus was almost impossible.

Perhaps an hour had passed when Megan and Robert found they were alone. "Want a Coke?" asked Robert. They were right in front of Pearl's.

"This is madness. Yes, I need a breather. Work some magic to get us a drink and a seat."

"You love Halloween, Megan. I know that." Robert ordered Cokes when they pushed out of the crowd and into the restaurant.

"Sort of." Megan laughed.

A very sad clown came up to the bar where they stood and looked at Megan. She wanted to cry with him, his manner was so woebegone. Instead she put her arms around him and whispered in his ear, "It's all right. Things will get better."

"If I look sad will you hug me?" Robert put on a long face.

"I only hug total strangers." Megan was amazed at her sense of abandon. But everyone seemed safe tonight.

They found two chairs near the big picture window and watched the crowd while they sipped their drinks and rested. Suddenly Megan nearly doubled over with a stab of fear. A cloud of pure evil filled her nostrils, cloying, clogging her mind and pores, her body with its nauseous smell. She choked on her drink. "Robert!" She grabbed his arm. "Bunny! Something has happened to Bunny."

"What—how do you know, Megan?"

"Never mind. I just know it." How could Megan explain that she had seen Bunny fall from the lamppost? The picture flashed through her mind so quickly she had trouble believing it herself. It was the same kind of knowledge she'd had when Cynthia fainted at the dance, only this time the clear picture was mixed with naked fear.

On the mall they heard the siren pierce the air. "Let's go, Robert. We have to hurry."

"There's no way we can hurry through this crowd, Megan." Robert tried to follow Megan, who was pushing people aside frantically.

The sheer number of people held them to a frustrating, creeping pace. Megan tried not to get angry and start screaming. That was what she wanted to do. By the time they reached the spot where they'd left Bunny and Roxie the girls were both gone.

A wizard filled them in on the details. "Suddenly she just fell, the silver fairy. Such a beautiful girl. The crowd caught her, so she wasn't hurt. She was unconscious, though. Her friend went with her to the hospital."

"I wonder where Derrick is," said Robert as they headed for the car.

"Forget Derrick. He won't care." Megan ran as fast as her floppy shoes would allow.

Starting their evening from the hospital, they'd

parked north of the mall, so now it was easier to get through the traffic jams to go back. Megan clutched the door until her hand ached, watching Robert inch his way to Broadway and turn right. They parked as close to the hospital as they could get. Megan jumped from the car and ran, not worrying if Robert was behind her, not worrying about what people thought of a clown racing toward the emergency entrance.

Bunny had been checked in through emergency, but her parents, living close to the hospital, had called their own doctor and were getting Bunny a room when Robert and Megan arrived.

"I almost didn't let her go out tonight. She hasn't felt well since before Homecoming. But the lovely costume. . . . And Roxie begged." Mrs. Browne looked as pale as Bunny had earlier, now that Megan thought back.

Roxie sat sobbing in a vinyl chair, her costume an incongruity with the sterile, Naugahyde waiting room. "Bunny said she didn't feel good three times. But I insisted. I don't feel so good myself, but I didn't want to miss the celebration. And we had these costumes." Roxie took a breath. "Will someone take me home?"

There was nothing Megan and Robert could do, so they took Roxie home. Then Robert headed for Megan's.

"Will you come in, Robert?" Megan invited. "I need some company. My folks went to a party."

Halfheartedly, they put a match to the fireplace, where a fire had been laid. The house seemed unusually cold to Megan. She'd gotten chilled in the late October air, despite long underwear and a sweater under her clown suit. Sitting on the stone ledge in front of the crackling fire, she cupped her hands around a steaming cup of cocoa. But she couldn't stop shivering.

Robert sat beside her and circled her shoulders with a warm hug.

"What's going on, Robert? Have we got some kind of mysterious epidemic at Boulder High?"

"Two people sick? I don't call that an epidemic. And I heard the mention of mono twice."

"I'd like to think it's mono. I need to think it's mono." Megan giggled despite her confused feelings. "But mono is contagious. You get it by kissing."

Robert pulled her even closer. She snuggled in the hollow of his shoulder, not worrying about getting her clown white on his jacket. He kissed her fuzzy head, then her ear, which had escaped the green wig. "Are you going to wear that wig forever?"

Megan tugged off the lime green hair and tipped her face, her painted-on smile, toward Robert, wanting him to kiss her. "I might have mono."

Robert took the cup from her hand, placing it on the hearth. "I'll risk it, but if both of us get sick, who'll report the epidemic?"

"Miss Hubbard?" Megan giggled. Their journalism teacher was single and would probably remain so unless her personality changed drastically. "I doubt she'll catch it."

"I've never kissed a clown before." Robert's lips closed over Megan's.

With the fire behind them and the warmth of Robert's kiss, Megan stopped shaking, but only until Robert spoke.

"What did you mean, Megan?" Robert

questioned. "When you said Derrick wouldn't care about Bunny?"

"I never said that."

"Yes you did. When we were looking for him. I feel guilty about leaving him. I hope he gets home all right."

Megan stopped listening to what Robert was saying. She didn't remember the statement about Derrick, but she knew it was true. Derrick didn't care what happened to Bunny or Cynthia. And she couldn't shake another idea.

One that was totally crazy.

He had something to do with it.

# Chapter 9

Megan talked her mother into going with her to the hospital Sunday afternoon, since a blanket of snow covered Boulder and the foothills. Megan didn't have much experience driving in snow. "You can get groceries or something, Mom. I won't stay long, but a phone call just isn't the same thing as being there."

She visited Bunny first. Bunny's blond hair fanned out across her pillow, and her face was pale. She appeared to be asleep, but when Megan stood there for a moment, Bunny's eyes fluttered open.

"Megan, hi. Thanks for coming." Bunny didn't try to sit up.

"How are you, Bunny?" A silly question, but what else to say?

"I'm okay, just weak. It was lucky people caught me or I could have been banged up good. It was funny. Suddenly I didn't have the strength to hang on any longer. I've felt strange for over a week now. Roxie's sick too."

"Roxie? How do you know?"

"She called me this morning. She's at home. But she says she feels the same as I do—weak."

"Cynthia's doctor thought it was mono at first."

Megan sat on the edge of Bunny's bed. She didn't mention the other tests that Cynthia had. She didn't want to scare Bunny.

"If it's mono, I know three boys, or maybe more, who'll have it soon." Bunny giggled, despite lying flat in a hospital bed.

"Get some rest, Bunny. I've got to see Cynthia, and my mom will have a fit if I stay all afternoon."

"Lay off kissing for a few days until we see what's going on," Bunny advised.

Megan laughed and headed out the door and down the hall. Then her smile faded. Cynthia seemed to be asleep. Her mom sat on the bed, holding Cynthia's hand. Mr. Harlow sat in a nearby chair. Cynthia's face was ashen.

Megan looked from Cynthia to Mrs. Harlow and then Cynthia's father. He answered the unspoken questions. "The doctors are confounded. The tests reveal nothing, but she's gotten worse since last night."

"We appreciate your cheering her up with the decorations, Megan." Mrs. Harlow tried to smile. The witch behind Cynthia's bed hung askew, the tape losing its stickiness. One streamer was down, crumpled in the corner. Cynthia's roommate was gone. Mrs. Harlow saw Megan glance at the empty bed. "Since the doctors didn't know what they were dealing with, they moved Geri out."

"Three girls are sick." Megan told them about Bunny and Roxie's illness.

Cynthia didn't wake up while Megan was there. After about ten minutes, she felt uncomfortable sitting there. No one knew what to say. So Megan excused herself and left, promising to stay in touch.

Megan's mother questioned her in the car. "Did any of you eat at the same place recently?"

"The school cafeteria. But if that's where this came from, everyone would be sick."

"Do you feel all right, Megan? I don't want to go on my trip if you're getting sick." Her mom had a modeling trip to the Caribbean coming up.

Megan felt awful, but it was mental, not physical. "I'm fine, Mom. Don't start worrying. I don't know what's going on, but I'm going to find out. I'm not a reporter for nothing. There has to be something in common with these three girls."

Three turned to six on Monday after the rumors were tracked down. Candy Gilford, Marva James, and Lora Santana were absent. All the Homecoming attendants were ill. So maybe the illness had something to do with the Homecoming festivities or a time that these girls were all together. Did they eat or drink anything in common during the ceremonies? Or during practice?

Before Megan could start any investigation, Mrs. Leffingwell, the assistant principal, called her in. Now what? Megan couldn't take much more trouble.

"Megan," Mrs. Leffingwell said, getting right to the point. The last three issues of *The Owl* were spread on her desk. "I'm not a fanatic about women's lib, but I'm not too happy with the trend your photography for the paper is taking."

"What do you mean, Mrs. Leffingwell? I feel that the photography for this year is excellent."

"It's not the quality of your work, Megan, it's the subject matter. Look. Beauty, beauty, beauty. Homecoming queens, attendants, two issues of that. Pretty girls in costume for Halloween. I know it's

58

news, and that it's the time of year for all this, but can't you balance it out with other photos—women athletes, women in the chem lab, not to mention some boys who aren't on the football team?''

"Mmmm, I guess you're right.'' Megan understood what Mrs. Leffingwell was saying. Not being one of the school beauties, she should have been sensitive to it herself. But she didn't expect to have her picture splattered over every page.

"I followed this a little farther, Megan.'' Mrs. Leffingwell placed a folder full of photos on the desk and spread them out like cards in a player's hand. "These are the recent photos that have come in for inclusion in the annual. The same type of photos, school beauties. Even all the informal shots are of these girls. There's not one photo of the student council president, Jolene Peterson. No photos of the girls' gymnastics activities, the other girls' sports this semester. Maybe you planned to take those later, but if you don't get some soon, those sports will be over.''

Megan studied the photos over Mrs. Leffingwell's shoulder. "I'm sorry you had to call this to my attention, Mrs. Leffingwell. I should be more aware in my job. Robert might not notice this, but I should. May I borrow all these photos so I can make a presentation to the staff in the morning?''

"Certainly. But return them to the annual when you're finished. They may want to use some of them—or even all, if they're balanced out with other pictures. Selections aren't anywhere near final yet. And I'm sure you'll remedy this problem in next week's newspaper.'' Mrs. L. smiled an I-knew-you'd-agree smile and dismissed Megan.

Megan's mind swirled with thoughts that were

trying to come together. She clutched the stack of slick, pasteboard images on top of her books and disappeared into the newspaper office. She'd cut her last two classes.

Monday was quiet, since the scramble to get out Friday's paper never started until after the staff meeting. Megan pulled out a sheet of notebook paper and spread the shiny faces before her. She started with a list. Cynthia, Roxie, Bunny, Candy, Marva, Lora. These were the girls that were sick. These were the faces she'd looked at in Mrs. Leffingwell's office, the ones that were spread before her.

She tallied the number of photos of each girl. Cynthia led the count, but there were several poses for each girl. Homecoming, Halloween, informal poses in the hall, the courtyard, the classroom. When had all of these been taken? Recently. When had the girls become ill? Just these last two weeks. Who was most ill? Cynthia and Bunny. They also led the list for number of photos taken.

Her hands shaking, Megan turned over each photo. The photographer's name was required on each. Quickly she glanced through the stack. All the pictures were by one staff member.

Derrick Ames.

None of the photos in the stack she had before her belonged to her or Robert. But what did that mean? Derrick had turned in his photos. She and Robert hadn't gotten around to it. Megan had taken photos of these same girls. What was she sitting here trying to prove? That because these girls had been photographed they'd gotten sick? No way. That was a ridiculous thought. It was simply a coincidence.

And why was she upset that Derrick's name was

on each of these particular photos? Why wouldn't they be? He'd been assigned all these jobs.

Then she remembered all the extra photographs Derrick had taken of Cynthia at the dance. He hadn't been assigned those. She thought of the look on his face when Cynthia had fallen ill, that grin.

You can't incriminate a person for his attitude, she told herself. For not liking someone or being angry at her. Her mind was trying to force an idea on her that was totally impossible. But something told her it wasn't. Just as she had known Bunny had fallen, just as she had felt that Cynthia was ill at the dance, she knew Derrick was behind the Homecoming Attendants' being ill. But how could she ever prove it? Unless she had some proof, people would just laugh at her.

A clicking sound caused Megan to jump. She shuffled the photos into a pile, covered them with her notebook. She was holding her breath when Robert entered the office and flicked on the light. She hadn't even noticed that the sky had darkened, promising more snow.

"Megan? What are you doing, sitting in here with such dim light? It's sixth period. Don't you have English?"

"I guess so." Megan forced herself to breathe normally.

"You guess so? What's wrong, Megan? You aren't getting sick, are you?" Robert sounded worried.

"No, no, I'm fine," she assured him. "Well, actually, I'm not fine. I've discovered something, Robert. Mrs. Leffingwell helped call it to my attention. Come here and look." She might as well try out her theory on Robert, see what he'd say. She spread out all the photos again.

"All the girls who are sick have been photographed an unusual number of times. And the photographer for all of these particular photos is Derrick."

"So? You and Derrick and I do almost all the photography work for the paper. And a lot of our pictures go on to the annual staff."

"I know that, but—"

"Those are the most popular girls in the school. You know there are always people who are photographed more than others. Especially the girls who are pretty. And we've just had Homecoming. Might it also follow that those girls are the ones who'd get mono, too?" Robert grinned, teasing Megan.

"That kissing business is a joke, Robert. Last year only two people in the whole school had mono. Harold Fox—who is not what his name would suggest. And Ruth Anne Penny—not the world's most popular girl. One was a freshman, the other a senior, and they probably never even sat side by side at lunch."

"Okay, forget the kissing joke, Megan. What could you possibly be getting at here? I thought you were my best reporter, and here you are thinking up something—well, I'm not even sure what you are thinking."

"I'm not either," Megan admitted. "But call it a hunch, Robert." Megan could see that she and Robert were poles apart. She sure wasn't going to mention that sometimes she *knew* things. It sounded too peculiar. "Call it woman's intuition. Something is going on here. I know it."

"Okay, don't get mad, Megan. Prove it to me

and I'll listen. Give me some concrete evidence that these girls have gotten sick because Derrick took their pictures. Or because we took their pictures. What are you saying? That the camera is stealing their souls?'' Robert started to laugh. And put into those words, it did sound impossible. Even ridiculous.

"Laugh all you like, Robert.'' Megan gathered her books and the photos. "I'll get you some concrete evidence if you insist.'' She pushed past Robert and started out the door.

Megan didn't like Robert or anyone else laughing at her. As farfetched as her idea sounded, she knew Derrick had something to do with this. There was some tie-in between the fact that he had taken an inordinate number of photos of Cynthia and Bunny, and that they were the most ill. Especially Cynthia.

"Megan, be reasonable!'' Robert shouted to her as she hurried down the hall.

"I am. You haven't heard the last of this.'' Tears filled Megan's eyes as she found her way to her locker.

Not caring who saw her, who knew she was cutting classes, she headed for the library, leaving the photos in her locker. Pulling books from the shelves, she settled at a table and read more than she wanted to know about mono. The final bell rang and she left the pile of books for a library assistant to shelve.

Hurrying back through the crowd, she reached her locker and grabbed her notebook and several books. She knew she wasn't going to study tonight, but she'd make the pretense. Swinging around to leave, she crashed right into Gus. Books, notebook, lunch sack with a leftover apple all tumbled to the floor.

"I'm sorry, Megan." Gus gathered Megan's books and piled them back into her arms. He looked at a photo of Cynthia that had escaped the stack in her notebook. His face was stricken with pain. "Want to go to the hospital with me?"

"Not today, Gus. Give Cynthia my love. Tell her I'll call her tonight."

Then, as Megan started down the hall, another voice made her freeze in her tracks. "You dropped this, Megan." Derrick handed her another photo that had slid away from her. It was an informal shot of Cynthia, obviously labeled on the back for the annual. A photo Megan should not have had in her possession.

"Oh, thanks, Derrick. I'm getting some shots of Cynthia blown up to poster size for her birthday. It's in November." Her voice trailed off as she met Derrick's steel gray eyes, intense, questioning.

"Want a ride home?" The tone of Derrick's voice had a magnetic pull to it, and Megan felt she couldn't refuse to go with him even if she had wanted to.

"Yeah, sure," Megan said quickly to show Derrick that life was normal and that she had nothing to hide from him. "I'd appreciate that. I've got tons of homework."

The trip to Gunbarrel Greens, their subdivision, started out as silently as their drives usually were. But again it was not a comfortable silence. Megan squirmed in her seat and longed to escape sitting there beside Derrick. She wanted to shout, "Stop!" and jump out of the van. Could Derrick feel her fear? She had a feeling he could. She wanted to throw up a shield between them, hide her thoughts, her emotions.

"Derrick?" Megan had to ease the tension. She'd try talking. "Remember when you said I had given you a good idea? Ready to tell me what it was?" She tried to laugh casually.

"I doubt you'd understand it if I did tell you about it, Megan," Derrick said.

"Now you're insulting my intelligence." Megan tried to tease, pretend she was offended by Derrick's remark. "Just because you're some kind of genius, doesn't mean you have the corner on intelligence. Try me. I might understand more than you know."

"I don't think so." Derrick really wasn't going to tell her anything.

"Come on, Derrick. If you tell me and I don't understand, then you can say, 'I told you so.' You have my permission. I thought you liked me. That we were friends." Megan kept talking.

Derrick stared at her while they waited for a stoplight. Then he turned his eyes back to the road.

Megan kept pretending that things were normal. "Pick me up tomorrow for staff meeting?" She opened the door when they got to her house.

"Sure, Megan. No problem."

She slammed the van door; then had to open it, slam it again. *No problem*. She hoped there wasn't a problem. Please, please, she thought as she ran to her door. Let Robert be right. Let me look foolish. Let me be wrong about this, whatever it is. Let me be wrong about Derrick.

# Chapter 10

By nine o'clock that evening Megan had a plan. It wasn't a good one, but it was the only one she could think of. She had to get inside Derrick's house, into his darkroom. She might find something there—what, she couldn't imagine, but something. A poisoned apple for the sleeping beauties?

Her mind had gone from rational thinking to silly, confusing theories all evening. If she could just stop her imagination from going in all directions until she had some more facts.

Even if she had to apologize to Robert, she needed him in on the plan. She dialed his number.

"Robert, I know you think I'm being silly, but go along with me, please. It's important. I need you to give Derrick an assignment so I'll know where he is for a couple of hours."

There was a pause at the other end of the line. Then Robert laughed. "Okay, Megan. I'll give him the city council assignment. He'll hate it. But we need someone there, since they're talking about school funding, possibly some remodeling at the high school."

"You'll insist he go?"

"Yes. I'll find a good reason why I can't."

Robert made good on his promise Tuesday morning. Derrick grumbled about having to go to the city council meeting, but in addition to the remodeling, a group of Boulder High's council was going to propose a joint city and school Renaissance festival. Robert wanted a report on both activities in the school paper. Megan had given him the word from Mrs. Leffingwell. He didn't like his paper being criticized and thought a picture of Boulder's woman mayor and Boulder High's female student council president would be good on the front page of the next issue. He assigned Jim to write up a serious election story to go with the photos.

The day dragged on. Megan's mind wasn't on school. She missed Cynthia. She ate her lunch alone in the newspaper office, looking over past issues.

School out, she dashed to the hospital to find no change in Cynthia. She was asleep and responded to very little, her mother said. So Megan didn't stay long. At dinner she said she had to go to the city council meeting and that Derrick was picking her up. She hated lying to her parents, but how could she explain to them that she had to break into Derrick's darkroom?

"Why doesn't that young man come to the door like a date is supposed to do?" Mr. Davidson grumbled.

"Because this isn't a date, Daddy. It's business."

"Business, ummmph." His eyes teased. "Monkey business."

"No, Daddy. This is really an important evening for our school."

That wasn't totally a lie. What Megan was doing

could be really important. She dashed out before he could question her further.

Fortunately, they'd had the harvest moon for Halloween and daylight saving time was over. Gunbarrel Greens was very dark. Since it was out of the city, there weren't as many streetlights either. Megan hoped if anyone saw her she would look like another teenager coming home from school late.

How was she going to get into Derrick's house? Some houses out here had burglar alarms. Police didn't make rounds often, so people took care of their own security. Would Derrick's mother be that cautious?

It turned out to be simple. Just before Megan reached Derrick's house, Mrs. Ames turned into their drive in her station wagon. Megan stopped behind a lilac bush at the curb of a neighbor's house and watched her get out of the car. To Megan's surprise, she was laughing. Then Megan heard a chinking sound and cursing. Mrs. Ames had dropped her keys. She mumbled as she searched. It was obvious to Megan that she'd been drinking. Footsteps told Megan she'd found them and was walking to the front door. Don't turn on the porch light, she willed. Seven o'clock. She glanced at her watch. Not a great time for breaking and entering, but the city council meeting started at seven, and Megan had no other choice. She might have two hours, less if the school representatives were scheduled first.

Slipping from the bush to the station wagon, Megan approached the house. If Mrs. Ames came back out, Megan would ask if Derrick was there. She'd have to hope that Mrs. Ames wouldn't later tell Derrick that Megan had come visiting. Megan clutched the cold casing of her flashlight. The graveled front yard crunched as she tried to cross it. The sound was like ice breaking in the evening's silence.

Megan's plan was to look in the windows, locate Mrs. Ames, and then start trying windows. She didn't need to. Mrs. Ames had left her key ring in the front door. Maybe she had stopped at a bar after work. Her drinking must have made her forgetful. Megan didn't hesitate. She turned the key, slipped open the door, and, seeing no one in the flagstone entryway, tiptoed through it and toward the stairs.

The distinctive sound of ice dropping into a glass and a beverage being poured reached Megan's ears. The shrill jangle of the phone made her jump and huddle on the first step. Where was the phone located?

"Oh, yes." Mrs. Ames's voice was still in the kitchen. "I had to stop and celebrate on the way home. I'll leave Sunday if I feel better."

Good—maybe she'd be tied up in a telephone conversation for a long time. Up the carpeted stairway Megan ran, toward Derrick's room. She hoped he hadn't changed rooms since she'd been inside the house. He'd been really proud of his darkroom and had seemed to enjoy showing Megan around at the welcoming party, which seemed so long ago.

Abnormally neat was her first impression as she circled the room with her light. Old-fashioned furniture, a bed with posts, a rolltop desk. Smaller than her bedroom, since Derrick had partitioned off some of the room; added it to the bathroom for his darkroom. She tried the bathroom door. Locked. Now what? Where would he keep a key? On his key chain, with him? Hidden in his room? Quickly, she searched the tray on his dresser. Some small change, a tie clip. Pulling out each drawer quietly, she shined her light.

Where would I hide a key, she thought. None of the drawers looked promising, and she felt funny going through piles of Derrick's neatly stacked underwear and handkerchiefs.

On one wall was a bookshelf with some books, some knickknacks. Shells from trips, a ship model, old Tonka toys. Megan smiled. Had Derrick really been a normal little boy, playing with trucks and jeeps?

For a moment she stopped to listen. Mrs. Ames would know Derrick was gone, since his van wasn't in the drive, so she'd be suspicious if she heard noises from his room. Then, standing on his desk chair, she ran her hands along the top bookshelves. At the very end was a large conch shell. She picked it up and heard a rattle. Holding the light between her knees, she took both hands and turned the shell upside down to let a key slide into her hand. She smiled. It had to be!

Leaving the chair in place so she could return the key, she ran quickly to the bathroom door. Yes, it fit. Her flashlight showed her dark shades on the only window. She snapped on the room's light to get her bearings, then flicked it off again. Turning around to the solid wall formed by the partitioned-off bedroom door, she gasped. There, arranged in neat rows, were dozens of photos pinned to the corkboard. All of them were duplicates of the photos she'd held in her hands so recently. But there was one difference. Around each girl's body was a glow, as if something surrounded or emanated from each person.

# Chapter 11

Megan studied the photos, running her light past row after row. Cynthia at Homecoming, many informal shots at the game and at the dance. Also Cynthia at the hospital with Bunny and Roxie. But there were more. With what had to be a telephoto lens, Derrick had caught Cynthia coming out of her house, in town, at school, informal shots, as if he'd followed her around. Photographs not assigned by either the annual or the newspaper. Photographs he'd taken on his own initiative.

Quickly, she glanced at the rest of the pictures on the bulletin board and the stack on the table in front of the display. All were of Bunny, Roxie, Candy, Marva, and Lora. All the girls who were ill. In one corner near the bottom of the groupings were four recent snapshots of Derrick's mother, obviously unposed, probably taken without her knowing. And his mom's face and body was surrounded by the same glowing light.

"I'll leave Sunday if I feel better." Megan remembered Mrs. Ames's comment to the person on the phone. Feel better? Derrick's mom wasn't feeling well? How did she feel? Weak? Or did she have a cold? Maybe her drinking was making her sick.

There was no real answer here to what was going on. Derrick had taken all these pictures—many more than he needed. And all of his subjects were ill. That was fact. Megan *knew* it wasn't coincidence, but this was no real proof. How did the photos work? Why had Derrick done such a thing? Megan had the evidence that told her Derrick was behind this. But absolutely nothing that would stand up if she were to go to the police or even accuse Derrick to his face.

Megan was used to seeing a camera and photographs side by side, so it took her a moment to register that one of Derrick's cameras was also in the darkroom. How many cameras did Derrick have? Megan searched her memory. She remembered Robert commenting on Derrick carrying two cameras, but she couldn't remember if he'd always carried two. Was this. . . .

She picked up the camera and examined it, turned it over and over. It looked like a normal camera, except . . . except. . . . there was no label on it. What brand was it? Didn't all camera manufacturers label their cameras? The camera suddenly felt hot to her touch, and she set it down quickly, as if it could burn her fingers.

Again she looked at all the photographs. She stared at Cynthia's smiling face. Anger started deep inside and crawled up Megan's spine until it reached her throat, choking her.

She tried to swallow it, push it down. Anger wasn't going to help her right now. She tried to think, be logical. Logically. . . . Megan stopped. None of this was logical. That was the problem. But if the photos somehow made the girls ill, would destroy Derrick's work make them feel better? If it did, she would at least have more evidence in her mind—still not concrete evidence, but proof for her idea. Maybe then . . . But there wasn't time to formulate a further plan now.

Quickly, with no more time to speculate on the situation, Megan started pulling the photos off the wall. She dropped the pins to the floor as she grabbed each pasteboard face. Click, click, click. When her fist was full, she piled them up and started another row. So many—a larger number of Cynthia, and Cynthia was the sickest of them all. But there were at least ten or twelve of each girl. Megan wished she had a sack, her backpack, anything. For a second she hesitated as she knelt at the bottom row. Then she grabbed the four pictures of Derrick's mother.

Clutching the awkward pile of photos, most printed on slick paper, Megan piled them outside the darkroom door, snapped off the light, and turned the key. Jumping on the chair, she returned the key to the shell, placed the chair back under Derrick's desk, and prepared to leave the room. Silly—he would know someone had been there when he saw the photos were gone.

In the hall, she hesitated. It took both hands to clasp the pictures to her chest. Pulling up the bottom of her jacket, she made a kind of pouch to help hold them. She could scarcely see and couldn't believe a house could be so dark. One flip on and off of her flashlight showed her the stairs. She started down. Then her foot slipped and she had to grab for the bannister. Fortunately, she didn't drop her light, but all the pictures slid downward with a soft rustle.

Damn. For a moment she froze on the second stair and waited. Had Derrick's mother heard? Would she investigate? Megan could tell her the story quickly, but would she believe it? She would believe she hadn't felt well—but that her son was doing it? No.

Snapping on the light again, she started gathering up pictures as fast as possible. Turning, she flashed the light up and down the carpeted stairway. Did she have them all? Quickly she stripped off her jacket and wrapped the photos in it. She couldn't risk dropping them again. Her light showed one picture in the downstairs hall. Cynthia smiled up at her as she grabbed it and added it to the pile.

She tied her jacket arms over the package and pressed it to her. She listened again. There was a tinkle of ice and the murmur of Mrs. Ames's voice. She was still on the phone. Thank goodness. Hurrying out the door, Megan had reached Mrs. Ames's station wagon when the lights of an approaching car lit up the street. The rattle and clunk was familiar. Derrick was home! She shuddered as she imagined those steel gray eyes on her as she knelt on the stairs picking up his photos.

Huddling into as small a heap as possible, she leaned on the right front tire of the wagon as Derrick parked on the street. The cold of the hubcap seared through her sweater. Without her jacket, she started to shiver. The slam of the van door echoed across the dark streets. Then there was the soft thud and crunch of his shoes on the flagstone walks and the gravel in between the stones.

She heard Derrick swear as he found his mother's keys in the door. He would take them in, find his mother on the phone, show her how careless she was

74

when she was drinking. And later he would realize how an intruder had found it so easy to get into his room. Megan didn't wait for that to happen. She ran.

Every thud of her tennis shoes on the walk echoed and made her imagine identical thuds behind her, following. She started to gasp for breath. After this was over, she'd need to lose the extra weight she'd never worried about. Maybe she'd need to take up running. But who could have known she'd need to escape from someone she'd thought was a friend?

Derrick might go straight to his room when he found his mother on the phone. He'd see the photos gone. Run to see if he could find out who'd been there. Would he immediately suspect her? He'd seen the photo she'd dropped from her notebook in the hall. Who else would he be apt to suspect? Had she left any evidence? He could easily run after her. He might have already started.

By the time she reached her house, she was gasping and crying and shivering. She leaned on the inside of the door until she caught her breath. Her dad sat in the family room before a cheery fire. Her mom hummed in the kitchen as she finished cleaning up after baking. Megan could smell the yeasty fragrance of bread and probably sweet rolls. When her mother didn't have a filming, she loved to stay up late. And she'd be baking things for them to eat while she was away on her trip.

Coming from her experience at Derrick's, Megan felt she'd entered another world. A safe one, she hoped.

"Home so early?" Dad looked up from his novel. "The boys are slipping."

"It was a meeting, not a date," Megan reminded

him. Her voice sounded hollow and breathy. "Good night. I have homework." She escaped before anyone could say, Why do you have your jacket wadded into your arms? Why do you look and sound as if you've run a race?

"Cocoa?" Mom called as Megan started upstairs.

"No, thanks." Megan had more on her mind than cocoa.

In her room she fanned out the pictures and looked at them again. They were just shiny prints of photographs in the light of her room. Negatives. I should have looked for negatives, she thought, forgetting the close timing of Derrick's return. Scooping up the stack of faces, she dumped them into her armchair, covered them with an afghan, and spread books on the desk.

But while she made the pretense of studying, her mind went over and over the new facts she had at hand. Six girls were ill. Derrick had photographed the six girls over and over. Maybe others were ill that she didn't know about. There were students who could be absent and no one would miss them. She made a list. Check absentees for the last two weeks. Ask Jolene Peterson, student council president, how she feels tomorrow after being photographed by Derrick at the meeting. That might prove that one of Derrick's cameras was normal, and that the one he'd left at home was the one that . . . that. . . .

Then another thought hit her. She grabbed the school's prints from her desk drawer and snapped off her desk light. From each print came the same soft glow surrounding each face and body. She scooped up the pictures and added them to the pile in her armchair. She'd think of some excuse for not returning them to the annual staff.

The house got quiet. Megan had turned off her light at ten. She felt strange sitting in her room in the dark, waiting, waiting. Finally, flipping on her lamp, she gathered the photographs in her wastebasket and left the room. She stood in the hall for a moment. No noise except the water gurgling in the hot-water heating system. The temperature must have dipped again. The heat had come on.

Downstairs, red coals lay in the fireplace, remains of the evening's cheery fire. Dad had shut the glass doors to keep cool air from entering the room later. Carefully, Megan slid the doors aside. She picked one photo from the basket and turned the corner into the coals, blowing slightly to make it catch fire. After a moment, flames licked merrily around Bunny's smiling face. Sure it was going to burn, Megan dropped the picture on the grate and took out another. As soon as she had a small fire going, each picture feeding on the flames of the last, she speeded up the process. Even then, it took her over an hour to be sure every scrap was gray ash.

Fatigue took hold as she closed the fireplace and stood. She ached all over and her eyes burned from smoke and lack of sleep. She didn't lie awake with the problems of the evening for long, however. Her body demanded rest. Her mind conceded.

She had not slept for long when she woke herself up, screaming. Smoke, fire was all around her. She was trapped. Her arms and legs were tied. She tugged and pulled, but she couldn't escape. The flames licked greedily toward her. The heat was intense. There was no way for her to escape. Derrick sat watching her, the tiny smile on his face.

# Chapter 12

"Megan, wake up!" This time it was her mother who shook her awake. Then she held Megan close while Megan sobbed. "Megan, oh, Megan, are you worried about Cynthia? You're—you're not getting sick, are you?"

"It—it was a dream, Mom." Megan didn't dare mention the airplane crash again. Her parents seemed frustrated with her because she couldn't forget it. But what was Derrick doing in her airplane-crash dream? It was the fire, the photos burning that set her off. Her subconscious added Derrick because of her fear that he was somehow behind the girls' being sick.

Mrs. Davidson stayed with Megan until she slept. Megan didn't dream again, but she woke feeling heavy, tired, as if she could sleep all day. That frightened her, too. If Derrick had been photographing Cynthia without her knowing it, he could get all the pictures of Megan he wanted as well. But she hadn't found any. No, she was tired because of the dream, because of staying up until her parents had gone to sleep.

"Oh, Mom, I'm sorry." At breakfast Megan took one look at her mother and knew she couldn't model that day. There were dark circles under her eyes and her lids were puffy.

"It's all right, Megan. I called and said I wasn't meeting my appointments. They can reschedule. It's you I'm concerned about."

"I'm fine, Mom, really I am. I guess I am worried about Cynthia."

"Look, I'm taking advantage of today to do some needed shopping. I'll drop you off at the hospital. Be late to school."

"That's a great idea. I have first period free anyway."

"I'll write you a note if you need one."


There were no formal visiting hours at Boulder's hospital and security was fairly loose. No one questioned Megan's being there so early. She went right up to Cynthia's room. To her surprise, Cynthia was sitting up in bed sipping some orange juice. She was still pale, but since the last two times Megan had visited she had been asleep, any improvement pleased Megan. Megan's mind quickly made a connection. Could burning the photos have made Cynthia's improvement possible?

"Cynthia, you seem better." Megan flopped in the orange plastic chair by Cynthia's bed.

"I do feel better. I gather I've slept a lot lately."

"Several days."

"Maybe I'm over the worst of it." Cynthia smiled. She was so thin. "Megan, would you stop by with assignments again this afternoon? I must be months behind."

"Are you sure, Cynthia? Wait a few more days."

"Please, Megan. I have to graduate. I'll only work as much as I feel like it."

"Cynthia, did you see much of Derrick after he asked you out and you said you wouldn't go with him? Not necessarily see him to speak to, but across the room or outside or anywhere?"

"Not that I recall. He came with you on Halloween, and, of course, he annoyed me a lot at the Homecoming Dance. I guess he hates me now. Poor Derrick. But that's his problem. You know, Megan, even if you are friends with Derrick, he gives me the creeps. He stared at me, probably getting up the nerve to ask me out, for weeks before he said anything. Why are you asking?"

"Nothing," Megan assured her. Why share all her theories with Cynthia, who needed to concentrate on getting well? "If he should come to visit you, will you call me? Immediately?"

"I don't think Derrick is going to visit me here, Megan. Do you?"

"No, but I want to know if he does."

"Are you jealous?" Cynthia said, teasing. Her eyes showed more sparkle than Megan had seen since Cynthia got sick.

"Of course not. I'm crazy about Robert. You're getting behind on that romance." Megan spent the rest of her visit talking about herself and school gossip, needed diversions from the hospital routine.

"Hey, I'm going to miss second period if I don't hurry. 'Bye, Cynthia. Keep getting better."

"I will," Cynthia promised.

By the time Megan got to school it was a quarter to nine, but she took time to stop in the office.

"May I see the attendance reports for the last of October and this week?" she asked Peter Wallace, the assistant at the desk.

"Sure, Megan. Working on a story?"

"Sort of. Attendance isn't very exciting, though. I'll have to think of something to go with it."

"Jolene Peterson is sick. The city paper has picked up on it." Peter held up the *Daily Camera*. MYSTERIOUS DISEASE HITS BOULDER HIGH, the headline read. "Health officials are with the principal now," Peter said. "They scooped you, Megan."

Megan grabbed the newspaper and scanned the article. It was general. Named those who were out ill. Saved Megan some time. Only the six girls she knew of were in the article. No fade-into-the-woodwork girls were sick. And, for some reason, they hadn't included Jolene in the story.

Megan glanced at the first-period reports for the day, since they were on top. Peter had just written them up. Her eye caught the name of Derrick Ames. Derrick had missed first period, too.

"Peter, keep your mouth shut and look up Jolene's address for me, will you?"

"Oh, I've got it. You *are* working on the source of the plague." He grinned and headed for a file cabinet. He returned with a scribbled address on a pad. "Funny it's only hit girls so far. I guess that helps prove male superiority, huh?" Peter grinned again. "Good luck, Megan. I'd love it if you scooped the local press and the powers that be."

Megan smiled, waved, and turned to leave the office. The heck with classes. She'd catch up later. Lamenting her lack of transportation, she ran for a bus and headed back to north Boulder. Jolene lived north of the hospital, but toward the mountains. Her mom answered the door and seemed surprised to see Megan.

"May I see Jolene, Mrs. Peterson? I'm a friend

of hers from school." Megan didn't know Jolene well, but Mrs. Peterson wouldn't know that.

Jolene sat in bed, reading. She was surprised to see Megan, too. "Hi, Megan. Cutting classes today?"

"Sure, why not?" Megan laughed. "Actually I'm trying to scoop the *Daily Camera* and track down the bug that's alive and well at Boulder High. How do you feel? Why are you home?"

"To tell the truth, Megan, the *Camera* called me, but I just have a cold. I was so tired when I got up. Well, it scared me. I'm a terrible hypochondriac. Also, I've had mono once, and I don't need to get it again. I figured a little extra sleep might be insurance."

"Then tell me about last night's meeting. I'll work on two stories at once. Did Derrick get some good photos?"

"I should hope so. He took enough. Several of me, of me and the mayor, me and the city council. Mentioned some stink about you only featuring beauty and not brains. I tried not to take that as an insult."

"Well, if the insult came from Derrick it doesn't carry much weight. He's put me down so often I'm used to it."

"I guess he doesn't worry about making friends. He's in love with cameras." Jolene laughed. "Get me some publicity, Megan. It might help me get a scholarship in political science."

"I will, Jolene, but answer one more question for me, and this is important." Megan didn't want Jolene asking too many questions, but she had to have a correct answer to this one. "Was Derrick carrying one camera or two?"

Jolene frowned in thought. "Just one. Why?" Before Megan could make up a reason for needing to know, Jolene got excited and kept talking. "Listen, the council thinks the Renaissance Fair is a good idea. We want to have it at Christmastime. An old-fashioned Christmas with carolers and jesters."

"And a roast pig?"

"Maybe we shouldn't go that far." Jolene made a face. "But we'll put the Madrigals on the mall in medieval costume—that sort of thing. Then a day of festivities at the school."

"Sounds like fun, Jolene . . . I'd better dash. I don't need too many teachers on my case."

In the forty-five minutes it took Megan to get back to school, she mulled over the new bit of information she'd added to her list. Jolene did appear to have only a cold. Derrick took only one camera to the council meeting. He photographed Jolene with that camera. The camera in the darkroom was his second. The one that did whatever it did to make the girls sick. She was sure of it.

During the rest of the day, she saw Robert a couple of times at a distance, but since he already thought she was nuts, she didn't want to try talking to him again until she had more facts.

Quickly gathering Cynthia's assignments, she made the bus trip back to the hospital. Cynthia's door was closed. A nurse stopped Megan as she stood wondering if she should knock.

"Are you looking for Cynthia Harlow?"

"Yes, what's wrong? I'm her friend. I've brought some homework. I saw her this morning. She was fine."

"She had a relapse. The doctor and her parents

are in there now. Why don't you wait out by our station? Maybe you can talk to her parents. No one else is allowed in. In fact, now that an article came out in the paper about a mystery disease, they've tightened her isolation. You may have to have a permit to visit. Frankly, I never thought she was contagious, but now we aren't taking any chances."

Megan couldn't believe it. Cynthia had been so much better that morning. Somehow she'd felt that burning the photos had made the difference. How or why she still had no clue, but it had worked. She knew it had. Or was she imagining it? She didn't know what to think. She slumped in a chair.

The nurse was friendly. Megan took advantage of that as her brain started to function again. Derrick was absent this morning. "Has anyone else visited her today—from school—someone beside her parents? Maybe before you tightened the quarantine on her room?"

"Let's see; I came on at two. Carol Andress is on the seven-to-four shift. She was getting ready to leave when old Mister Stelmach started yelling for attention. She's the only one who can please him. You can talk to her in a few minutes."

Megan couldn't sit still. She started to pace the floor. What had happened? Could Derrick have just printed more photos? If Derrick's taking pictures of the girls was the source of the illness, was it the initial photograph? Or the prints? If he had stayed home and made a lot of new prints, would that have hurt Cynthia? Megan couldn't believe what she was thinking was possible, but she had enough facts to support the incredible fantasy she kept dwelling on.

The blond nurse named Carol Andress was kind, too. "We were so glad Cynthia was better. No one knows what happened to make her relapse. Bunny and Roxie improved a lot today, too. They are begging to go home. We'd decided the disease, whatever it is, had run its course."

"Were there any visitors here this morning?" Megan asked again. "Any guys? These girls are incredibly popular at school." Megan pretended to laugh.

"I can see why. All three are gorgeous creatures—even when they're sick." The nurse thought about Megan's question. "Sure. There was a young man here with a camera. I stopped him, thinking he was from the newspaper. After that article came out in the paper we were watching for reporters. He said he was from the school paper, but wasn't here on business. That he was a good friend of Cynthia's. And since we didn't really have her in quarantine, I saw no reason not to let him go in to see her. He said he always carried a camera from habit. Offered to leave it with me if I was concerned about it. He was awfully sweet. Do you know him?"

Megan made sure. "Did he have kinky hair and wire glasses?" Megan knew the answer. Gus never carried a camera, and Robert wouldn't have come.

"Yes, that's him. We've gotten to know Gus, but this was a new visitor for Cynthia. She has lots of friends that have come by. So do Bunny and Roxie."

"You moved Cynthia's roommate. Why haven't you stopped visitors if you think this disease might be contagious?"

"To tell the truth, we've kept debating it with the doctor. Since he can't find anything medically wrong with any of the girls, and since visitors help so much, we haven't been careful. If it is mono, it's hard to catch.''

"You still think it's mono?'' Megan asked in amazement. "But you can't diagnose it?'' Modern medicine wasn't looking too good to her at the moment.

"We've even checked for that old Legionnaires' disease. Don't print this, but the doctors are baffled. I imagine that, with Cynthia worse this afternoon, the order will come through for a complete quarantine.''

The order would be too late for Cynthia. Megan sat on the couch to wait and see Cynthia's parents. But she now accepted her idea fully. The nurse's confession that the doctors couldn't diagnose the illness and Derrick's visit to Cynthia convinced her that her theory was the truth. A strange truth, but nonetheless real. Derrick had come to the hospital, taken more photos of Cynthia, and now she was worse. Obviously, it was the initial photo that did the dirty work, somehow sapped the girls' life energy. Otherwise Derrick wouldn't have risked coming to the hospital. He would have printed more photographs from the negatives he had.

Megan couldn't sit and do nothing. She walked back to the nurses' station. "What rooms are Bunny Browne and Roxie MacNeil in? The same room Bunny had earlier?''

"Yes, they're sharing 311.'' The first nurse was at the desk again. Carol had disappeared. "We're keeping all the Boulder High cases isolated. Are you sure you should be visiting them? A no-visitor policy is sure to come through now that Cynthia has gotten worse.''

"I was with them before they got sick,'' Megan

assured the nurse. "And I've visited Cynthia every day. I was exposed to all of them, and I feel fine. I'm sure I'll be all right."

Megan headed down the hall toward 311. Pushing on the door, she walked in, surprised to see both Bunny and Roxie sitting up in bed, watching a game show on TV.

"Hi, Megan. Are you still well? How's the newspaper business holding up without us?" Roxie said.

"We miss you both. I'm having to do all the work. You're lots better, it seems, both of you."

"Yeah," Bunny answered. "I felt like eating this morning. I might not be able to dance all night, but I'm tired of this place. I'm ready to go home."

Megan got right to the point. "Bunny, did Derrick say anything to you when he was taking pictures. About anything?"

"Well, he doesn't say much, you know."

"Yes, I know. But did he say *anything?* Roxie, do you remember?"

"He did tease me some," Roxie said. "I remember because I was so startled to have him talk to me at all, other than 'Stand here, move there.' "

"What did he say? Tell me exactly?"

"Megan, are you jealous?" Bunny laughed. "I thought you were in love with Robert."

"How can you even think of falling in love with Derrick?" Roxie asked with a gasp.

"Play them off each other," Bunny said, eager for some boy talk. "Let's give her some advice, Roxie."

Dating was the farthest thing from Megan's mind. But Bunny and Roxie had been going out since junior high, and Megan knew they were eager to share their experience.

"Hey, I'm not falling in love with Derrick, or even thinking of going out with him. I do like Robert," Megan explained. "But I'm curious about Derrick. He's such a character. I'm thinking of doing a sketch on him for the Senior Sketches column."

"He's sure different from anyone I know," Roxie agreed. "He asked me if I didn't worry about being photographed so much."

"Me too." Bunny giggled. "He said, 'What if the camera could steal your soul piece by piece.' Isn't that a riot? He sounded so mysterious."

Bunny and Roxie laughed at the idea. Megan didn't.

"He laughed, too," Bunny said. "I've hardly ever seen Derrick laugh."

"Me either," Roxie added. "It was weirdsville. And after he stopped laughing, he kept smiling that funny little smile as he took more pictures. It gave me the creeps."

"How's Cynthia?" Bunny remembered to ask. "The nurse said she was better today too."

"I'm going back now to find out. She's not doing as well as she was this morning." Megan didn't want to worry Bunny and Roxie, who seemed almost back to their normal selves. But she did feel she needed to warn them. "One more thing, if Derrick should come to visit you, promise me you'll call a nurse."

"Derrick visit us? That would be super weird. You *are* jealous, aren't you, Megan?" Bunny laughed. "Everyone to her own taste, huh, Roxie?"

"Right. You and Derrick, Megan? Nope, stick with Robert."

Let them think she was jealous. "Okay, maybe I am. Derrick and I have a lot in common, and I like creative people. But promise me you'll ring for the nurse immediately if he comes in here."

Megan left, hoping they'd take her seriously. Why hadn't she told Cynthia to call a nurse if Derrick came to see her? But she never dreamed that Derrick would be daring enough to walk into the hospital and photograph Cynthia right there. Or that he was that vindictive. He had reason to dislike Cynthia, but what about the rest of the girls? What did he have against them? The more Megan found out, the more puzzled she became.

Mr. Harlow was in the hall with the doctor. Megan waited until they finished talking. Then she felt like she was intruding when she approached Mr. Harlow. He seemed far away. But she had to know.

"Mr. Harlow—Cynthia— What did the doctors say?"

"Megan, oh, Megan." Tears flowed down Mr. Harlow's cheeks. "He thinks we're losing her. There's hardly any pulse, and she's been unconscious since noon."

Cynthia dying? No. No! Megan sat down. She put her head in her hands to keep from sobbing out of control. It wasn't possible. It wasn't!

# Chapter 13

A nurse—Megan didn't know her name—sat beside her. "Maybe you'd better go home, Megan. There's been no change for hours. Your parents might worry."

Megan looked up. It had gotten dark and was almost six o'clock. Her watch ticked away the seconds. Time—Cynthia needed more time. Megan needed more time to solve this situation. She went to call her parents.

"Megan, where are you? We've been worried sick," her mother said.

"I'm sorry, Mom. I'm at the hospital. Cynthia is worse, and I lost track of the time. Can someone come and get me? I'll wait at the entrance."

Megan's mother said her father would come. As Megan waited, thoughts of what she could do for Cynthia bombarded her brain. She had to do something. She was the only one who knew what could save Cynthia, but would anyone believe her? Her dad? Should she tell her father? Robert? She had told Robert in the beginning and he didn't believe her, but she had to talk to someone.

After dinner, when her parents were quiet, respecting her worry, she went to her room and dialed Robert's number. Once, twice, three times. Be there, be home, Robert. She knew he was home. He answered on the fifth ring.

"Robert, I need to talk to you. Right now. Please don't say no. I need you."

"Megan, I have a math exam tomorrow, but I confess you keep coming between me and my studying. I can't stop thinking about you. Are you all right?"

Megan was tired of people worrying about *her*. She needed to find someone to help her worry about Cynthia, about Derrick.

"I'm fine, Robert, but Cynthia isn't. The exam isn't important. Leave it and come—no, meet me at the hospital. In the lobby."

"Is Cynthia worse?"

"Yes, she—she—may not make it." Megan couldn't bring herself to say the word *die*. It was something that old people did. Megan's grandfather had died. He was the only person she'd known who had.

"Okay, Megan. I'll see you in a few minutes."

"Mom, Dad, I know neither of you wants to go back out, but I need to get back to the hospital. Can I have the car?"

"I don't want you driving in this state of mind, Megan," her mother said. "I'll take you. Are you sure you want to go back, Megan? What can you do just sitting there?"

"I don't know, but I have to be there. Cynthia is worse. Robert will bring me back."

"Do they have any more ideas about why Cynthia is sick?" Mrs. Davidson asked.

"No, the doctors are baffled." What would her

mother say if Megan told her what she thought was wrong with Cynthia?

"Do you want me to come in with you?" Mrs. Davidson asked when she stopped the car to let Megan out. "I don't want to be in the way, but—"

"No, Mom. I'll call if I'm going to be late, and Robert is coming over."

Robert wasn't in the lobby. Megan found him pacing the floor in the intensive-care waiting room. Megan looked at his face and knew. "Megan, I just checked the desk."

"She's gone." Megan realized she'd known it before she saw Robert. She'd known it the minute she walked into the hospital. A picture had flashed into her mind. Cynthia, cold and pale, lay in a bower of cut flowers. All the flowers were white. Cynthia was in her Homecoming dress. So beautiful. She looked so beautiful, as if she were sleeping.

For a moment Megan stood, staring at nothing, trying to accept the fact that Robert had confirmed.

Robert took her in his arms. "I can't believe it, Megan. She was so young, so alive."

Megan wanted to cry, but no tears would come. She felt as if someone had punched her in the stomach and she couldn't react. She couldn't bend over, curl into a ball, be sick.

"Why, why did Derrick do this?" Megan whispered. "It couldn't have been because Cynthia turned him down for a date. Boys don't kill girls just because they say no to a date."

"What are you talking about, Megan?" Robert pushed her away and looked at her. "Derrick didn't do this. You can't believe that idea you told me about earlier. That's impossible."

"It's not impossible. Derrick killed Cynthia," Megan said aloud. "He did this. I don't know how, but he did." Hysteria was starting to build inside Megan.

Robert surely sensed it. He pulled her toward an elevator. She let herself be led outside, and then she went to pieces in the parking lot.

"Why won't you listen to me, Robert? Cynthia's dead! Derrick killed her. I can't prove it, but he did."

"I know you're upset by this, Megan, but forget that crazy idea. You're just hysterical."

"I'm not hysterical," Megan screamed, giving the lie to her denial. She tried to calm down. "Last night I went to Derrick's house. I got into his darkroom. He had a whole wall of photographs—all of them the girls who are ill. In all the photos a funny, weird light surrounded the images. There were more of Cynthia than of anyone. I took the pictures home, Robert. I burned them. Last night I burned them. This morning Cynthia was better. So were Bunny and Roxie. And I know the rest were, too; I just haven't had time to check."

Robert kept his hold on Megan, but he was shaking his head. "Megan, of course Derrick had pictures of all those girls. He'd taken them for the paper and the annual. Maybe he'd pinned them to the wall to study his technique. I do that all the time. You know Derrick is always trying to improve his work. He mentioned to me once that he might become a fashion photographer. This is something you've dreamed up. You've imagined it because you were upset by Cynthia's illness."

"I haven't imagined this, Robert." What could she do to convince him? "The extra camera, Robert.

Derrick started carrying an extra camera. Remember when he missed two days of school? Right after that he started carrying another camera, and he used it to photograph the ceremonies at the game and the Homecoming Dance. Remember, Cynthia fainted at the dance. I saw the camera, Robert. He didn't take it to the city council meeting. He didn't use it to photograph Jolene, and she's fine. I checked on her again to be sure."

"Lots of photographers carry two cameras. I would if I could afford another. Cynthia was always high-strung as well as delicate. Anyone could look at her and see that. She was stressed and exhausted. Whatever she had was coming on and she didn't have the strength to fight it. They're looking for a virus now, Megan. I talked to a man from the health department today. I haven't had time to tell you."

"It's not a virus!" Megan started to cry. She sat down on the curb beside Robert's car, curled into a ball, and sobbed. "If it were a virus I'd have it and you'd have it and Gus would have it," she said, when she could manage to speak again.

"Megan, let me take you home." Robert tried to pull Megan to her feet.

"I can't just go home and do nothing."

"What do you want to do? Let's go across the street and get some hot tea or coffee. Go over this story again. I promise to listen. I won't say you're crazy."

Megan knew Robert was humoring her, patronizing her, but what could she do? Maybe if she thought it through again she could explain it so he'd believe her. She got to her feet and let Robert lead her across the street from the hospital where there was an all-night coffee shop.

94

Digging a handkerchief from her purse, she wiped her eyes, blew her nose, and tried to get control of her emotions. Robert ordered two cups of coffee. They came, steaming hot, the rich aroma tempting her. She took a few sips carefully. She would never convince Robert if she kept being hysterical. She could feel Robert's eyes on her, concerned. He did care. About her. But he didn't believe a word she was saying. She kept staring at the brown liquid, drinking it slowly, letting it warm her inside. If she could ever feel warm again.

Finally, looking up, she blinked her eyes. Once, twice, to try to clear her vision. Derrick's face floated before her. He was out there, by the front windows of the coffee shop, staring at her, smiling, holding a camera, pointing it at her. She gasped and blocked a scream.

"Robert, there. He's there—outside the window. Derrick. Right now."

For a second Robert froze, staring at Megan. Then he jumped up, dashed to the front door, and slipped outside. When he came back, his eyes were kind, pitying Megan. He didn't believe her. He thought she was imagining things. Was she? Did she really see Derrick? Or was it a hallucination? Or— or one of her visions? Because she was upset, because she was thinking of Derrick, had she imagined his face watching her?

"There's no one out there, Megan. I looked in both directions and even walked to the corner. All the stores are closed except the coffee shop. Hadn't you better get home? I'll take you."

"I can't go home, Robert. I can't forget this, no matter what you think. What if we drove by Derrick's house? We could even talk to him, tell him about Cynthia. We could say we wanted to do a memorial section of the paper for her. Ask if he'd share his photos. Any story we can think of. If I can see his reaction, if I can be with him, I'll know. I'm sure I will."

"Would that make you give up this crazy idea you have about his involvement with Cynthia's death?"

Cynthia's death. . . . Cynthia's death. . . . Megan had to fight to keep her control at hearing the words, taking them in.

"No, but I might feel better. It's something to do. I don't know what to do, Robert. If you won't believe me, no one will."

Robert paid for the coffee and they stepped out onto the sidewalk. Megan couldn't help looking both ways and around the parking lot of the small shopping center. There were almost no cars. The place was deserted. Wouldn't Derrick's van be in the lot if he were here? No, he'd hide it.

She put her mind into neutral, tried not to think. She let Robert guide her across the street and put her into his car. They were silent on the way across town, out to Gunbarrel Greens, to Derrick's house. Robert switched on the radio to late-night, new-age electronic music. It should have been the dreamy end to a date, Megan snuggling close to Robert, listening to the soothing sounds.

Derrick's house was dark. Neither his van nor his mother's car sat in the drive. They had a garage. It was closed. Megan insisted they ring the doorbell even though it was late. Over and over she pushed it, as if the act would produce Derrick or some answers to this deadly puzzle.

"He's not home, Megan. No one is home."

Robert took her hand and pulled her back to the car. "Look, tomorrow I'll ask him to go on the photo trip. The industrial sights, remember? We'll spend one day with him this weekend, and have time to ask questions. Okay?"

"The funeral will probably be this weekend." The word jumped into Megan's mind. White flowers, white dress.

"Okay, next weekend, Megan." Robert didn't say more, but turned the car around and drove to Megan's house.

Again Robert helped her from the car and led her to the house. Megan went along, hardly knowing he was there. He probably came in with her, turned her over to her mother. She had a vague sensation of her mother putting her to bed. Of drifting off to sleep.

Suddenly before her there was a deep, dark hole. She walked to the edge and peered down. Way below was a bower of white flowers. Cynthia lay atop them. A pearly white light came from the hole. Slowly, magnetically, Megan was pulled into the hole. She tried to step back, to grab someone, Robert, anything. But she felt the cold, dampness. She reached out and touched the waxy petals of the lilies. She smelled the sickeningly sweet flowers close around her.

# Chapter 14

"Megan, do you want to go to school today?"

Megan came awake with her mother gently shaking her. "What? How'd I get to bed?"

"You fainted, honey, remember? Robert helped your father get you up here. You came to, but you kept talking about Cynthia. We felt it was better to let you sleep. It's noon, though, and I needed to go to town. I didn't want you to wake up alone."

"Cynthia. Mom, Cynthia is dead."

"I know, baby, I know. Robert told us. Are you all right? You're not getting sick, are you?" Megan's mother sounded panicky. "What is this sickness that's hitting everyone?"

"Not everyone, Mom. Just a few girls." Everything came in on Megan, and she lay back down. "No, I'm not sick. Can I ride into town with you?"

"Maybe you should stay home today."

"No, I don't want to lie here and think about it." Megan might discover another piece of this puzzle at school. And she didn't want to stay home alone. She wanted to see Robert, the school, the other kids, to reassure herself everything was still there. That there was some part of life still normal, if that was possible.

Her mother had brought her a croissant with butter and a pot of tea on a tray. She sat up and forced it down, then felt a little less wobbly. She slipped on a pair of jeans and a sweater, not caring how she looked.

Being at school wasn't much better than staying home alone would have been. Everyone was talking about Cynthia. They kept looking at Megan and would stop talking or whisper if she came close. Several of her friends came to her and expressed sympathy. Megan mumbled to them, not really aware of what she was saying. She didn't see Derrick or Robert until after school.

Derrick came up to her. "I'm sorry about Cynthia," he said, staring at her as if he dared her to deny his statement, to accuse him of not being sorry at all. Was she wrong about all this, after all?

"Thanks, Derrick." What else could she say?

"Isn't this yours, Megan?" Derrick held out a hair clip, an enameled butterfly. "Did you leave it . . . somewhere?"

Before she could stop herself, she reached up to where tendrils of her hair, too short to reach her braid, were pinned back by similar-style clips. "No, that's not mine, Derrick. Where did you find it?" She stared into his gray eyes, dared him to say. She had to look away, but not before a shiver ran the length of her spine. And not before the tiny smile came to Derrick's lips. He knew, she thought. He knew she'd been in his darkroom. But he couldn't prove it.

She turned and ran from Derrick when she saw Robert. He took her home, neither saying more than polite, necessary phrases. Even his question, "Are you all right, Megan?" seemed polite, as if he didn't expect an answer. "Yes," she said, and ran to the house.

The rest of the week was just as bad. On Saturday she sat through the funeral service for Cynthia, hardly hearing what the minister said. The casket was closed. Megan was glad. She didn't want to see her friend lying there—no, the shell of her friend. Cynthia was gone. She'd remember the way she looked at Homecoming, all shimmering and happy on Gus's arm.

Gus sat two rows in front of Megan, uncomfortable and almost unrecognizable in a dark blue suit. His folks sat beside him. Gus's father was an older version of the football star. Gus would look just like him someday.

Megan's mom and dad sat with her and Robert. After the services Mrs. Davidson said, "Megan, I want you to go home with us. You look so peaked and tired. I can't help but worry."

"Your mother and I are taking a week off, Megan. We're taking you up to Vail." Mr. Davidson took Megan's arm and ushered her out of the church. "No arguments. It's all settled."

"That's a good idea, Megan," agreed Robert. "I'll cover all your jobs." He smiled down at her. "And when you get back we'll go on our photo session in Denver. I'll have it arranged."

Megan was operating from some kind of thick fog. She heard all that was said around her, but little registered. She let her parents take care of her, and before she knew it she found herself in a small cabin in the resort. Reality was pushed away for a week. On some level Megan knew this. On another she didn't care. It was only when she got back home that feelings returned.

At school on Monday Robert announced that he'd arranged their talked-about, but postponed, photographic trip for the next Saturday. She wanted more than anything to say she didn't want to go. But she had to go. She had to be with Derrick to find any more clues that might link him to this horror.

On Friday night, safe in her room, alone, she allowed herself to think. Megan had looked for Derrick at the church, but of course he hadn't been there. No murderer would go to the funeral of his victim.

Calling Derrick a murderer seemed a bit heavy now, more farfetched than it had when Cynthia died. She'd be with him tomorrow. Would she be able to tell by looking at him, being with him, if he was guilty? Would she have a flash of insight, one of her times of knowing something for sure? What if she just out and out accused him? "Derrick, did you kill Cynthia? Kill her by taking a lot of pictures of her?" The absurdity of the whole thing started to nag at her. Robert was right. How could she have believed such a thing? She'd built this big fantasy on a lot of perfectly normal facts, coincidence, and her imagination.

By Saturday Megan didn't really feel like running all over Denver's industrial and heavy downtown construction taking pictures. She didn't even want to get out of bed. Where was her enthusiasm? She mentioned it at breakfast.

"I suspect you're somewhat depressed, Megan, even if you don't realize it," her mother said. "Depression causes a person to feel tired. I'm trying to stop worrying about your getting this illness. Today's paper says there are no new victims."

There. Her mother had used the word. But, then, you could be the victim of a disease, the victim of an accident, as well as the victim of foul play. Megan needed to see Derrick to put her mind to rest that she had let her imagination get away from her. She knew she'd be able to tell if anything was really wrong with him. As strange as he acted, his behavior was consistent.

"I'm glad, Mom. I'd have hated for you to miss your trip."

Mrs. Davidson had been looking forward for months to the Caribbean trip. She'd be modeling all the new spring clothes. Packed and ready to go, she was catching a noon flight from Denver.

Robert had arranged for Derrick to pick Megan up. That was only common sense, since it was more convenient. They'd meet Robert at the parking lot at school and take Robert's car. His car was more reliable than Derrick's van.

Derrick drove up and honked the horn at nine o'clock. Megan didn't exactly bounce out to the van, but she was ready. "Morning," Derrick said.

"Good morning, Derrick." Megan had made a plan the night before to keep Derrick talking as much as possible throughout the day. He might slip and say something, anything, that would give her a clue. "Well, according to the paper the Boulder High epidemic is over," she said. "Doesn't it seem strange that no boys got sick?"

"Yeah. Too bad about Cynthia." His voice held no emotion, just fact. Too bad it rained. Too bad your car broke down, you got a bad grade, your friend died.

Megan couldn't think of anything else to say, and suddenly her mind was bombarded with thoughts of

Cynthia: slumber parties, the time Cynthia made them matching German peasant outfits for Halloween. What had suited Cynthia's personality looked ridiculous on Megan. Cynthia had to restyle them so that she wore the knickers and suspenders and Megan the full skirt and dirndl. Of course, everything looked good on Cynthia—had looked good on her. She could have been a model easily. Megan thought of the drawings Cynthia had been making for her spring wardrobe. Now the clothes would never be made. She rubbed a tear from her eye. She didn't want Derrick to see her crying.

Robert's presence helped. They switched to his car, Derrick in the backseat. Robert kept a running conversation going all the way to the city. He talked of black-and-white photography, a new camera he wanted, two new contests he'd heard about— shoptalk. Megan had never heard him chatter so.

They parked in an all-day-for-three-dollars lot on the edge of Denver, splitting the cost three ways. Walking to the area of cranes, steel girders and foundations, heaps of dirt, no one talked. The silence wasn't comfortable. This trip was a mistake, Megan realized.

They split up and looked for shots on their own, but Megan kept her eye on Derrick. He seemed totally absorbed in his work. She took a few halfhearted snaps and then worked her way closer to Derrick. He was carrying both of his cameras today. He'd set both cameras on a low, flattened heap of debris while he got out new film, rewound and loaded.

Megan wondered what kind of reaction she'd get from Derrick if she asked about the second camera, the one she suspected of . . . of. . . .

Quietly, she reached for the camera with no manufacturer's label. "Let me see your new camera, Derrick. I'm thinking of getting a second. What brand is this one?"

He grabbed her hand and thrust it back. Then he lifted the camera, throwing the strap around his neck. "You know I don't like anyone touching my equipment." His eyes met Megan's. What she saw there was hard, cold anger, but it was well controlled. For a moment she held his eyes and experienced the intensity of his emotions. She read them as well as if she'd been in his body. So Derrick did have emotions. She felt herself being choked by his anger, as if Derrick had hold of her neck and was squeezing, squeezing.

"I forgot, Derrick. I'm sorry." She looked away first, rubbing her neck. She felt as though he had struck her. He had never looked at her with such disgust, such hatred. It was so obvious that she could almost reach out and touch it, taste the bitter flavor.

Then he seemed to relax a bit. "It's just like my old one. I keep black and white in one, color in the other."

From one other trip the Photography Club had made early in the year, Megan knew Derrick liked to be left alone to shoot. She'd never deliberately violated his space before. She wanted to press him for more information about the camera, but suddenly she was afraid to stay near him. Right here in broad daylight, with Robert in calling distance. She was disappointed in herself.

She moved away and tried to get interested in some good subject matter. Looking back, she found Derrick's eyes on her. Now she read nothing in the stare, which frustrated her. She moved farther away, then glanced around. Derrick had picked up his second camera. His picking up a gun couldn't have been more frightening. Where was Robert? Suddenly, she wanted to run, find him, to be near him, stay close to him. It was all she could do to keep from shouting his name.

Robert had been lying down. When she saw him stand up, she fled to where he peered through his viewfinder.

"What's wrong, Megan?"

"Oh, Derrick gives me the creeps."

"He never won any popularity contests *before* you got that crazy idea about him. You were the only one who ever felt comfortable with him. Guess he's lost his only friend," Robert said somewhat teasingly, perhaps testing Megan. He smiled at her, and hugged her with one arm for a minute.

"So now I've joined the world?" Megan fingered her camera lens cap, snapping it on and off.

"'Fraid so. The world here, Derrick over there. Makes me glad I'm in the norm as far as being brilliant—well, I am brilliant, but no genius. You know what they say about that fine line between genius and—"

Megan cut him off. "Insanity." She pretended to laugh and sat on a pile of dirt to watch Robert. He took a couple more shots and then waved to Derrick to suggest moving to another site. Just as Derrick reached them, a voice called out.

"What do you kids think you're doing?" A policeman walked up from behind them.

"We're photographing for a contest. Black and white." Robert started chattering about camera clubs and art photos until Megan stopped listening. She'd leave it to Robert to talk them out of any trouble they might be in. Then she looked at Derrick. He stood beside her as rigid as a statue in City Park. His hand was tensed on his 200-millimeter lens.

"There are no trespassing signs everywhere," the policeman pointed out.

"We're staying mostly on the edge of the construction," Robert argued.

"Doesn't matter. You shouldn't be here."

Robert started to protest again. Megan put her hand on his arm. "It doesn't matter, Robert. Let's get some lunch and go to City Park. We might get some good geese and duck shots."

Megan would have expected Derrick to protest more vigorously than Robert. Robert was usually calm about any problem. But Robert seemed nervous today. First his nonstop talking on the way down, now this protesting when they were clearly in the wrong. There *were* signs everywhere.

"Let's go to the zoo," Megan suggested on the way back to the car. It was a beautiful day, sunny and warm, pure Indian summer. The day-after-Halloween snow was forgotten.

"I don't like being made to feel guilty when I've done nothing wrong." Robert was still talking about the policeman.

"Let's go home," said Derrick. "I have other work I can do."

Megan watched, unable to say anything, as Derrick pointed his long-distance lens in the direction of the retreating policeman. Two, three, four shots clicked off before he stopped shooting.

Robert agreed, so Megan's zoo trip was outvoted. It was probably just as well. She felt even more tired than she had that morning. She'd worked to keep her spirits up, and she could feel herself letting down.

An uneasy stillness filled the Camaro on the way home. Megan tried to think, to say something. She managed a couple of technical questions, but she didn't have the energy to keep a conversation going by herself. The morning's depression had come in on her, making her feel encased in a fog, in a quagmire of swirling questions and emotions.

"Want a Coke, Megan?" Robert asked when they reached the school.

"I thought you and Derrick had work to do."

"I do, but I'll delay it for a few more minutes." Robert flashed a smile at Megan that made her wish they were alone. "Okay, Derrick?"

Megan looked around. They were alone. Derrick was striding toward his van, forgetting that Megan and Robert existed. "There goes my ride home."

"No problem." Robert laughed then. "I'll admit I'm glad."

They went to What's Up and found a table that looked out onto the mall.

"I'm sorry about today, Megan," Robert apologized. "Even though I think you had a crazy idea, I think you've gotten to me. I didn't feel comfortable with Derrick. And to be frank, I'm worried about you. You didn't take any pictures."

"My mom thinks I'm fighting depression. I just feel tired in general. I guess it's normal."

"Please don't get sick, Megan." Robert took both her hands in his.

"I promise." She laughed. "After all, Derrick hasn't photographed me. Lucky I'm no school beauty, huh?"

"Here we are, two ordinary-looking, average, but super-talented people." Robert teased her.

Having Robert care about her was the only good thing to have happened this semester. She needed to hold on to that. "You know, Robert, I think Derrick hates beautiful women. I've seen him looking at Bunny and Roxie, and he plain doesn't like them."

"I don't think you can generalize. Maybe he doesn't like Bunny and Roxie as people. Hey, why are we talking about Derrick? He's gone. And I'm glad for some time alone with you to make this day better. Are you going to be okay—about Cynthia?"

"I already miss her terribly, but yes, I'll be okay. Having you for my friend, Robert, helps a lot. Let's take some photos on the mall. You aren't really in a hurry, are you?"

"Not anymore." Robert grinned.

Megan got permission from a watching parent to take some pictures of children riding the stone animals on the east end of the Boulder Mall. For a few minutes, she became a child herself, laughing with them, doing funny things to make them laugh at her camera.

Then, just as she sat on the back of a white marble bunny, all her strength seemed to leave her. Quickly, she put her head between her knees to keep from fainting.

"Megan!" Robert was beside her instantly. "Megan, please, please don't be sick." He held her tightly. "Tell me you're not sick."

Bunny's words flashed through Megan's mind. *Suddenly I couldn't hold on to the lamppost any longer.* Megan felt no pain, but a total draining of her energy.

"Fight it, Megan, fight it," Robert said all the

way to the car. He kept his arm around her, almost carrying her.

Megan was scared, really scared. She had been wrong about Derrick causing people to get sick. He hadn't taken any photos of her. There really was a disease, and now she was getting it.

Her father was home alone, having returned from the airport. Her mother had left that morning for her Caribbean trip. Mr. Davidson helped Robert get Megan up to bed.

"I'm going to call Dr. Bartlett," her father said, his voice in some kind of tunnel.

"Please don't call Mom," Megan mumbled. "I'll be okay, I know I will. Don't spoil her trip."

Megan lay back on her pillow gratefully. She was tired, so tired. Her bones felt heavy, her flesh like molten lead, which settled and solidified on the cool sheets. Her mind flickered up and back, up and back, like a candle flame in a mild breeze. All of a sudden, her consciousness latched on to one clear picture.

Derrick snapping pictures of the policeman without his knowing it. Derrick's hand, tensed on his telephoto lens.

# Chapter 15

Megan knew she'd slept all night, but that her mind had been a kaleidoscope of dreams. Derrick photographing her mother. Robert saying "Fight" and offering her a camera. Children standing before her with their big eyes saying that the white rabbit did it. Get off the white rabbit. Cynthia, shimmering in her white dress, saying, "Go back. Fight. You can do it."

Her dad dozed in Megan's over stuffed chair. He'd sat beside her all night. When she opened her eyes and stared at him for a minute, wondering what he was doing there, he woke up.

"Megan, baby. How do you feel? Dr. Bartlett came over yesterday afternoon, but you were so sound asleep he said to leave you alone. He'll come back or put you in the hospital for some tests."

It took all of Megan's strength to sit up. "Yes, yes. I'm better, Daddy. I was only tired." She didn't want to go to the hospital. She didn't want anyone worrying about her, either, but she knew her dad had been really worried or he wouldn't have sat by her bed all night.

"You didn't call Mom?" Megan asked.

"Not yet, sweetie. Should I? I don't want her to

return unless it's really necessary. Maybe what I'm saying is that I don't want to believe you're sick, sick enough to tell her. Robert called twice last night. He asked me to call him the minute you woke up today. Do you want to call instead?''

"Yes, I'll call him in a few minutes. And thanks for not telling Mom. Can I have some orange juice?'' Her mom couldn't help her now. Neither could Robert. Could she help herself?

When her father went to the kitchen, Megan willed herself out of bed. It had never seemed so comfortable. She was dressed when he returned.

"Are you sure you should be up?'' He handed her the juice.

She sat on the edge of her bed to drink it. "Yes, I'll be all right.'' She had to be. She had to find out. Last night she'd thought of Derrick's telephoto lens. He had taken pictures of Cynthia at a distance. Why not of her? She had to get back in his darkroom somehow to find out—to destroy the pictures if they existed.

Did she have to wait for tonight? How was she going to get in? Sunday. It was Sunday. If she could wait for tomorrow, Derrick would be in school. Tomorrow. As soon as she decided she couldn't get into Derrick's lab until Monday, she felt like lying back down.

Almost immediately she was asleep. The smell of perfume, Cinnabar, filled her nostrils. Cynthia was floating, shimmering in a swirl of clouds. "Go back, Megan. Go back!''

"Cynthia? Is that really you?'' Megan reached out to touch her friend. The clouds swirled and billowed up, covering the image.

"Megan. You don't have to come here. Fight. Go back."

Megan ran toward Cynthia, every step slow and difficult, as if she were in a slow-motion film. She wanted to go with Cynthia. It would be so easy to go. Robert's hand touched her shoulder.

"Megan, please wake up. You keep crying out, but I can't get you to wake up."

Slowly Megan focused on Robert's worried face. "Oh, Robert. Hold me, Robert. Hold me close. I'm so cold."

Robert put his arms around Megan. After a minute the warmth of his body crept into hers. The chill she felt gradually disappeared.

"You were dreaming about Cynthia." Robert kissed her cheeks, her temple, where her hair lay flattened by sleep.

"No, she was here, Robert. Here with me. She told me to go back. What do you think she meant?"

"I've read that when people die, their friends or relatives come to help them over. Cynthia sent you back, Megan. She sent you back. Please don't die, Megan. I couldn't face that."

Megan hugged Robert closer. "I'm not going to die." To herself she added, Because I'm going to destroy Derrick's pictures of me.

"I've been so worried about you," Robert said. "Your father said you slept all day."

"All day?" Megan struggled to sit up. It was dark outside. She had slept all night and then all day Sunday. She'd never done that before.

"Would you like something to eat?" Robert stood up, ready to go get Megan some food.

"Funny, I'm not hungry. But I would like a cup of tea. Strong and hot, with one spoon of sugar."

Megan usually took her tea or coffee unsweetened, but she felt the need for something to restore her energy quickly, if that was possible.

Robert stayed after he brought the tea, helping Mr. Davidson prepare hamburgers, bringing a tray to Megan. She ate half a hamburger, but it tired her to eat, to sit up. She never mentioned her fatigue, though. Just said she wasn't hungry.

"If you aren't better by morning, Megan," her father said, "I'm slapping you in the nearest hospital and calling your mother."

"Is that a threat?" Megan smiled.

"No, it's a promise. I should have put you in for tests yesterday. Apparently all the others who are sick started out by feeling tired, the same as you. And Robert said both Bunny and Roxie are back in the hospital."

"Okay, Daddy. But let's wait until morning to decide." Bunny and Roxie sick again?

"Take a couple of days off from school, Megan. You need it." Robert talked about the newspaper for a few minutes, taking Megan's mind off herself. Then he kissed her and turned to leave. "I know you'll be all right, Megan. I know you'll fight this. I can feel it. I feel closer to you than I ever have."

"I will, Robert. I promise I'll fight." Tomorrow, Megan promised herself. Tomorrow I'll fight. I'll go to Derrick's. See for myself if this is a real sickness or . . . or . . . what?

Waking from another twelve hours of deep sleep, this time with no dreams that she could recall, Megan felt soggy and restless. Eight o'clock, but not very light. Megan turned toward the window and found the cause of the dim light. It was snowing.

The sky was dark, overcast, and fine grains of pearlized snow pelted the ground.

"You're feeling better, aren't you, Megan? You look better." Was her father trying to talk her into being better, as Robert had done the night before? She felt no better, not rested for all her time in bed; but then, she felt no worse.

"Yes, I'm hungry. Can you manage a soft scrambled egg and a cup of tea?"

"Coming right up." Mr. Davidson smiled and hurried off to the kitchen.

Megan stumbled toward her bathroom and a hot shower. That was what she felt she needed. She let her anger take over, anger that Derrick could do this to her. The anger sent adrenaline coursing through her body, giving her the strength to shower, dress, and appear normal by the time her father appeared. She had even put on a little makeup, rouged her pale cheeks.

She sat at her desk to eat breakfast, hating the sight of her bed. Then she insisted she go downstairs for a second cup of tea. Loading the cup with sugar, she grimaced at the sweet taste. She needed a sugar high, any high, just for an hour.

Then her dad solved the problem of her getting away from him to go to Derrick's.

"Megan, would you be all right for an hour or so while I go down and get some papers at my office? This snow is supposed to keep up, so I'd rather go in before it gets too slick. I can easily work at home for a couple of days, but I need some files and my appointment book."

"Sure, Daddy. I'll be fine. I don't think I'll go to school, but being here alone is no problem.

Thanks for not calling Mom. I'll bet she's enjoying the sunshine. Envy, envy.''

Her dad gave her a big hug, put her into a big chair in front of a cheerful fire, and tucked an afghan around her legs. She sat, sipping the second cup of tea. She hoped she looked settled, comfortable enough to convince him she'd stay right there while he was gone. He had the TV news on, and she pretended to be interested in that.

She waited until she heard the roar and hum of her dad's Honda fade away. Not even bothering to turn off the TV, she tossed off the afghan and headed for the hall closet and her warmest coat. Just in case it was super-cold outside and she had to wait in front of Derrick's house, she had dug out her long underwear when dressing.

Having planned while she showered, she now walked slowly to her dad's downstairs office. She crossed her fingers that his cigarette-pack-size tape recorder was there and not in his office in town. She was in luck. Taking it from its case, she tucked it into her flannel shirt pocket, the on-off switch at the top of the flap. If she got into Derrick's house and needed to, she could turn it on to get evidence.

Getting inside was going to be the problem. If Mrs. Ames was there, and the only way she could get in was to lie to her, she had a story. She'd tell Derrick's mother that Derrick had called her and asked her to bring in some photos when she returned to school at noon. She'd talk her way out of whatever situation arose. She was determined to get into Derrick's darkroom. Once inside, it would take only seconds to grab any pictures of herself and the ones she suspected she'd find of Bunny and Roxie. Now she knew that the two cameras held the answer. One was normal, the other . . . Whatever it did, it worked. It was the one doing the damage. Derrick's second camera had the ability to make people ill—to steal life.

Even prepared for the drop in temperature, Megan gasped as she stepped outside, leaving the door unlocked so she could get back in quickly if necessary. November's preview of winter was piercing. By the time Megan had walked one block, she wasn't sure she could go on. Stopping, she took a deep breath. The icy air didn't replenish her oxygen, it burned her throat and lungs instead.

Waves of dizziness washed over her. She fought the blackness of sleep that was so desirable. "Fight." She remembered Cynthia's words, Robert's commands. "Fight!" she said aloud, as if it were a mantra or a school cheer, egging her on beyond her endurance. Then, anger at the possibility of this being Derrick's fault helped her again.

She planned to approach cautiously, but Derrick's van was not in sight. Mrs. Ames's car sat as if it had been parked all night. It was dry underneath, and icy snow was piled up across the windshield and between the bars on the luggage rack. Her plan to say that Derrick had sent her seemed sound. Mrs. Ames knew her. She rang the doorbell. Then, pulling off her glove, she punched the button again in case it hadn't functioned with her padded finger. No answer. She tried the knob. To her surprise, the door opened. Was Mrs. Ames drunk so early in the day? Was she always so careless? No one in the suburbs, or even in town, left doors open in this day and age.

Quietly, she stepped inside, pushing the door shut behind her. She stood there, breathing in the warm, stuffy air, resting for a moment and making sure the house was empty. Then she heard a soft moan.

A weak voice called out. "Derrick, is that you? Please, Derrick, help me."

Megan froze, as if the winter blast had penetrated the solid oak behind her. Something in the voice sent chills over her. She felt faint and nauseous. Get hold of yourself, Megan. You have a plan. Was Mrs. Ames sick or drunk? Megan would find out and then tell her story.

Mrs. Ames was lying on the brick-colored sofa, one hand dangling onto the soft cream carpet. She clutched an afghan to her chin, her fist tight over it, skin translucent so that the bones stood up in parallel rows, contrasted with blue veining.

Her hair was matted. Her makeup looked garish on her thin face, which was contorted into a grimace. Her eyes settled on Megan, the same steel gray eyes of Derrick, but missing the look of arrogance. What they held instead was fear. Mrs. Ames was afraid, and her fear transferred to Megan immediately.

Whether she was drunk or ill was not an issue. At that moment, Mrs. Ames was terrified.

# Chapter 16

"Megan, Megan, help me. Derrick . . . Derrick.
. . . Why, Megan? Why does Derrick hate me so
much? What have I done to make him hate me? I
wasn't responsible for his father leaving me, if that's
what he thinks. I've done the best I could. Why
does he hate me?"

Whatever Megan had expected Mrs. Ames to say,
it was not this speech. Having no answer, Megan
took precious minutes to try to help the frightened
woman.

"What's wrong, Mrs. Ames? Are you ill? Can I
call a doctor? An ambulance?" While it was coming
Megan could search the upstairs. Then maybe she
could ride along with Mrs. Ames to the hospital.
She'd be safe in the hospital. But Cynthia hadn't
been safe in the hospital. Megan could call Robert,
or her father. Show them the evidence she knew she
would find upstairs.

"I'm so weak. I can't get up. And Derrick . . .
He keeps laughing and taking those nasty pictures of
me. Why would he want a picture of me when I'm
ill? I must look a mess." Mrs. Ames pushed her
hair back with one thin hand.

"How long have you been sick, Mrs. Ames? Were you sick before Derrick took the pictures?"

"I don't know. Does it matter? I can't get up, and Derrick won't help me. He hates me. Why does he hate me, Megan?"

"I'll call an ambulance, Mrs. Ames." Megan started for the kitchen, where she knew she'd find the phone. Hurry, she needed to hurry. This was taking too much time.

"No, no, that's not necessary. Just help me. I'm sure I'll be fine if I can get up. I need to wash my hair and fix my face. I couldn't possibly go anywhere looking like this. And Megan, if you could pour me a little of that sherry. Over there in the cabinet. I'm sure that's all I need to get me on my feet."

Megan hesitated. Should she call the ambulance anyway? Help Mrs. Ames up? Get her a drink?

"Please, Megan. Just get me a drink." Mrs. Ames pleaded with Megan. Maybe she was only drunk. Megan would look foolish calling an ambulance.

Leaning over the woman, Megan pulled her to a sitting position on the couch. She smelled of expensive perfume and liquor. The exertion made Megan aware of her own weakness. She stopped to catch her breath. Then she ran to the liquor cabinet that Mrs. Ames pointed out and returned with a bottle of sherry and a glass. Mrs. Ames grabbed both, and although her hand shook as she poured, she didn't spill a drop.

"Derrick sent me here to get some photos for the newspaper." Megan remembered her planned speech. But suddenly the explanation seemed full of holes. She had no car. Derrick did. Why didn't he come back for the photos?

Mrs. Ames neither noticed nor seemed to care. She nodded and poured another drink. Megan left her and headed for Derrick's room. Twice she had to stop on the stairs to rest. Her mind urged her to hurry. Her body refused. Outside, snow pelted the window on the staircase landing as the storm grew worse and the wind picked up.

Inside Derrick's room, Megan noticed that the darkroom door stood ajar. She was relieved that she didn't have to climb for the key. So tired. She was so very tired. She felt like the saggy baggy elephant of her childhood reading days. All her weight pulled heavy skin, which sagged to the floor.

Fumbling for the light, she snapped it on. She turned to the cork-covered wall where Derrick displayed developed prints. Pinned to the wall like insects on display were a dozen snapshots of herself. Sitting on the rubble heap at the construction sight, getting into Robert's car, earlier photos at the hospital the night Cynthia died, one in the coffee shop, another coming out of her house. She ran to the light switch, flicked it off. All the images of herself were surrounded by that glowing light.

She was right. My God, she was right! By some process with his camera, Derrick was causing the mystery disease. He was responsible. He *was* Cynthia's murderer!

No more time to think, Megan. You have to get out of here. Get the pictures. Get out! Quickly she snatched the pins that held up the photos, dropping them to the floor with a slight snicking sound. There were three photos of Derrick's mother, lying on the couch, crying and waving at Derrick to stop. Megan grabbed those, too. When she got home she'd call the police, no matter how silly they'd think she was. There were the photos and the illness, the weakness. Surely someone would believe her.

She whirled, headed for the darkroom door. The surge of adrenaline caused by her discovery would get her home. But at the bedroom door, her hopes were dashed.

Derrick leaned on the frame. He smiled the funny little smile.

"Hello, Megan. I've been expecting you. In fact, I thought you might come yesterday. You've kept me waiting."

He waited? All day yesterday and today, knowing she'd come? The open door, the ease with which she'd gotten into the house and the darkroom was a trap. He wanted her to come in. For a moment Megan couldn't speak. She felt drained and faint again. She held on to a desk chair to keep from passing out.

Derrick wore the camera around his neck. Atop it was a flash attachment. Now he raised the viewfinder to his eye and snapped a photo of Megan leaning on his desk chair, holding the evidence she needed.

Megan blinked her eyes. "Stop, Derrick! Stop that! Why are you doing this?"

Leaning far over on the desk chair as if she couldn't stand, surreptitiously she reached her hand into her shirt pocket and snapped on the tape recorder. How sensitive was it? Would it pick up Derrick's speech from across the room?

Derrick didn't speak. He raised the camera again.

"Don't!" Megan screamed, covering her face. What good would it do to hide her face? The camera still photographed her body, her image, placing it on the negative, doing the damage that Derrick had designed it to do.

"Leave me alone, Derrick. You killed Cynthia. I don't know how, but I know you're responsible for this disease. Only it's not really a disease, it's you—somehow, it's you. I've guessed it for a long time, and now I know."

"I realized that, Megan. That's why I've waited for you. I knew you were suspicious of me. You came here before, didn't you? Bunny and Roxie said you warned them. 'Stay away from Derrick,' you said. You're interfering with my plan, Megan."

"What plan, Derrick? Why are you doing this? How far do you think you can go with it?"

No answer. The tiny smile. Then he said, "As far as I want to go, Megan. I'm in control now. You thought I was a nerd, didn't you? You and Cynthia and all the girls. Now what do you think?"

"I never once thought you were a nerd, Derrick." On the contrary, Derrick was a genius. Some kind of warped genius. He had thought all this out. He had been in the hospital again, or had he found Bunny and Roxie at home? Somehow he had photographed them again. Maybe they were right now dead or dying. How did the camera work?

Megan had to get Derrick to talk some more. "How does the camera work, Derrick? You were really smart to figure out something like that. Tell me how it works."

No answer. Again Derrick lifted the camera. Megan stumbled toward him, feeling totally without strength, but reaching out toward the deadly invention. Derrick grabbed her hands, and the photographs spilled to the floor.

"You must be a great admirer of my work, Megan, to keep taking samples home for your personal enjoyment." His fingers tightened on her wrists, cutting into her flesh. "Trespassing is a crime, Megan. I'm surprised at your breaking the law so blatantly."

The tiny smile. It was a cat-and-mouse situation. Megan felt the mesmerizing fear that a mouse must feel staring into a cat's whiskers. Held down by a furry paw. She tried to buy some time, time to think, work out another plan. She'd keep talking.

"Your mother is ill, Derrick. She needs your help."

Derrick laughed out loud. The sound echoed through the quiet house, cocooned now by a softer-falling snow. "My mother needs help, all right, but not mine."

He pushed Megan back to the desk chair. Then, as if he had this all planned, he reached into a desk drawer for a length of rope.

"Derrick, please don't do this. You'll never get away with it. *You* need help."

He tied her arms together in front of her, then her feet. "Shut up, Megan, or I'll have to gag you. You wouldn't like that."

"I don't like *this*. You're crazy, Derrick. Crazy!" Megan caught herself. She must not panic. Her only hope was to talk Derrick out of whatever he had planned. And she wanted to get as much conversation as possible on tape.

"Why did you kill Cynthia, Derrick? What had she ever done to you?"

Instead of answering, Derrick went into the darkroom, taking the spilled photos with him. He liked the place neat. Megan marveled at his cleaning up, just as she imagined he always did. He came back with two lights and placed them beside Megan's chair. Then he rolled the chair a bit as if he didn't like the background. Adjusting the lights, he turned them on. The glare made Megan blink. He was preparing her for more photographs, as if this were a portrait studio and she were a client. Oh, Derrick, you really are sick, she thought. She could see no way out.

He moved the lights inch by inch and then carefully adjusted the heads so they lit up Megan's face the way he wanted. He worked without speaking, but with a professional touch, as if she were a fashion model. He could have been preparing a spread for a magazine. Taking the camera from around his neck, he placed it on a tripod and pointed it toward her.

Fascinated, horrified, Megan had forgotten to argue with him. She had forgotten that her only chance was talking him out of this. She forced herself to speak.

"Derrick, haven't you done enough damage? Surely—"

"You're not the kind of model I like, Megan. But you'll have to do. You're not very pretty. Do you know that? I usually photograph only beautiful women."

"You took pictures of your mother." Keep him talking, now that he'd started.

"My mother was once beautiful. I remember how beautiful she was when I was little. But she's no good now, always drinking, going out with any man who'll have her. You're right, Megan. Having brains is better than being beautiful. What good is a woman who is only physically beautiful? Look at Bunny.

124

What good was Bunny to the world?'' He moved a light another inch and then peered through the viewfinder.

*Was?* The past tense. My God, was Bunny dead?

Megan spoke again, her brain trying to think, to focus. "Cynthia wasn't dumb, Derrick. She was smart and talented. She was more than beautiful.''

"But she didn't like me, Megan. She hated me. She embarrassed me. I don't like people embarrassing me.''

"She didn't hate you. She was in love with Gus. She couldn't go out with anyone else.''

"I think she hated me. You should smile now, Megan. You're much prettier when you smile.'' Derrick clicked the shutter closed. Megan started to struggle. All she could do was move her head.

"Be still. You must be still. I think you ruined that shot, Megan. I'll have to take some more.'' Over and over he moved and snapped pictures of Megan. All the while he gave her directions.

"Move your chin to the right, Megan. Just a little. Now look at me. How about a profile? Oh, not a very pretty nose. Too bad. Turn the other way. That's better.''

On and on he fussed and babbled, more than Megan had ever heard him talk. He seemed totally absorbed in the process. He gave her directions, but he didn't care that she didn't follow them. He changed to a 135 portrait lens and stayed hard at work, as if this were a serious session.

Megan's eyes felt heavy; her chin kept dipping toward her chest. Twice she perked up, trying to stay conscious, trying to think, to fight. "Fight this,'' voices reminded her. She had no fight left. Then, distinctly, she heard Derrick say, "Out of film, Megan. Would you excuse me for a few minutes?''

So polite. He continued to be so polite, so professional.

She forced her eyes open to watch him leave the room. Megan still wore her down coat. The lights were hot, and again she fought to keep her eyes open. If she went to sleep it was over. But she was sleepy, so sleepy. She dozed, jerked awake, dozed again.

"Wake up, Megan. Surprise."

Megan had been down a long tunnel. She heard Derrick's voice echo with a hollow tone. Fight, she willed herself. Fight to come back.

Her eyes fluttered open and she tried to focus. Derrick stood in front of her, grinning. "They really aren't as bad as I'd thought. If you knew how to use makeup, you could cover those freckles, bring out your cheekbones." He held several dripping, shiny photos before her. The face that looked out was frightened at first. Then it settled more and more into a stuporous look.

"Oh, sorry, the lights. You're too hot." Derrick snapped off the big photographer's lights. In the dim light she could see. Around her head and body in each of the photos was the glow, the light, as if something were either escaping from or surrounding her.

"See, this one is the best." Derrick held up one shiny pasteboard.

The girl in the photo smiled at Megan, a tiny smile she hadn't remembered. Was it automatic? Did everyone feel obligated to smile when confronted with a camera?

"I have to go now, Megan. You've had enough

of my time. My time is getting more and more valuable, since my work is progressing so nicely. Don't bother to call out. Mother is asleep, or dead drunk. You shouldn't have given her the sherry." He smiled again. "But I don't think she could have helped you anyway." Derrick went back to his darkroom for a few moments. Megan wiggled and tugged at her bonds, but it was no use.

"Actually," said Derrick, returning, "it's too bad you're so smart, Megan. It got you in trouble. And I liked you, Megan. I really liked you."

"Wait, Derrick. Where are you going?" Megan's tongue felt thick. Her speech was slow and slurred. "Don't leave me here tied up." She struggled with the few ounces of strength she could summon.

Derrick took his camera from the tripod, snapped it into a case, and placed it around his neck. "Bye, Megan. You realize I can't let you go now that you know. And Mother has gotten to be such a burden. I'll make it look like she did this to herself. People may wonder what you were doing here, but you won't be able to explain it to them. They'll just have to keep wondering. 'So sad. Such a tragedy. Megan was such a nice girl. Everyone liked her.' Go back to sleep, Megan. It will be easier." Slipping the tripod over his shoulder, he left the room. Megan heard him go down the stairs. She heard the front door click closed.

Again she shook her head, trying to will herself some strength. She felt heavy all over. Her head was heavy, her eyes . . . Easy . . . Let go . . . Easiest way . . .

Even when she smelled the smoke, it didn't seem to matter.

# Chapter 17

Thoughts swirled through Megan's head. Derrick's mother saying, "Help me, Megan, help me. Why does Derrick hate me?" Robert's smile. "Fight, Megan, please fight it." And Cynthia, always Cynthia, shimmering and beautiful in a soft glow of light. "Go back, Megan. I love you, but you don't belong here. Fight! Go back."

Megan opened her eyes slowly, and immediately started to cough. Smoke filled the darkroom and curled its long fingers into Derrick's bedroom. Fire! Derrick had set the house on fire in an attempt to destroy Megan and all she knew. She had to get out! But how? She struggled with the cords around her wrists.

"Help me! Someone help me!" Even to her own ears her voice sounded weak and soft. No one could hear her. And who was here to help? Mrs. Ames? Why hadn't she called an ambulance for the woman? She hadn't, though. And Mrs. Ames was in no condition to come to Megan's rescue. It was up to her.

Her dream about the airplane crash popped into her mind. It had been no dream. She had seen this,

this horror she found herself in now. She was tied, trapped, and soon flames would flick around her.

Megan coughed, feeling the smoke sting her eyes. Tears ran down her cheeks. The fire crackled as it licked up photograph paper. Then a soft *pop* suggested a bottle of chemicals exploding.

Her feet were tucked up onto the base of the office chair. Now, straining, she was able to touch the floor with her toes. She pushed. Inch by inch she worked the chair over to the bed. By the time she got there, she felt as if she had run a mile. Her legs ached and her toes cramped. Reaching out her arms, she hooked the cords that were around her wrists onto the knobs at the foot of the old-fashioned bed. She tugged until her wrists burned, red, raw, but the rope would not slip off.

Through her tears and the haze of the smoke-filled room, she saw now that snow was falling in soft, fluffy flakes. The world was quickly being covered with a blanket of white. The evergreens outside Derrick's window started to droop with the cottony covering. Megan felt she would like to get a picture of it, the wintry wonderland scene. She blinked and forced her mind to stop wandering. Acrid smoke filled her nose. She wasn't going to take any more pictures.

"Fight, Megan. Go back. I don't want you here." The smell of Cinnabar mixed with the smell of smoke.

Megan shook her head as if to clear the smoke from her brain, the smoke that filled her mind, clouding her thinking. She wasn't attached to the chair. Inching her hips forward, little by little, she leaned forward. Catching herself as best she could, she bumped the bed and fell onto the floor. The chair skidded out from behind her, softly rattling across the carpeted floor. Her coat had padded her fall, but the jarring hurt. She lay still, dozing. No. No! She shook her head. She couldn't sleep now. Like an inchworm, she scrunched forward, together, then forward again. She pushed her knees against the rug and scooted.

Surely this was not her body, but that of some elephant baby or a whale out of water. She slumped, her cheek against the short nap of the blue carpet. I have blue carpet, she thought. I like blue carpet. She shook her head again and rubbed it against the fiber until it stung. She didn't want to die on blue carpet.

The air was better on the floor. She must think only of good things. When I get out of this, I'll lose some weight. If she had a tiny, little body she could wiggle faster, easier. She started to giggle.

"Stop it, Megan. Stop it. You must stay in control. You are in charge here. Fight!"

Megan fought to control the wave of hysteria that threatened to engulf her. Down on the floor the smoke was not so thick. She took deep breaths of the better air and started to inch toward the bedroom door again. Using her tied-together hands, she pushed against the carpet to get a grip and then pulled herself forward. Stretch out, scrunch up. Stretch out, scrunch up. As she made progress, she began to gather strength and hope that she could get out.

But it was getting hotter. The fire crackled behind her. She felt perspiration pour down her body. Her head bumped wood. The door was closed. Please, Derrick, you didn't lock the door.

Pushing herself to a kneeling position, she twisted the knob with both hands. With relief, she felt it turn. The air was fresher in the hall, but opening the door allowed the oxygen to feed the flames behind her. Fire licked around the darkroom door frame. Megan felt encouraged by getting this far. She could get out. She'd crawl down the stairs and then out the door if she couldn't reach the phone in the kitchen. Her energy seemed to be returning with her forward progress.

Of course. The fire had burned the photos of her that Derrick had returned to the darkroom. Had he thought of that? Had he given her this small chance to escape? He hadn't tied her to the chair. And he had to know that destroying the prints would give back his victims some of the strength the camera had taken from them. Or had he slipped up in his hurry to destroy Megan and all the evidence? Had this one flaw in his plan escaped his thinking in his haste to cover his actions?

There wasn't time to wonder. Megan reached the stairway and started to crawl backward down the steep, rough-carpeted stairs. She grasped the low shag with her fingertips, not wanting to chance rolling to the bottom and maybe lying there injured as the flames crept down to the first floor.

She was about halfway down when she heard the doorbell ring and pounding at the front door. Someone was there. Who? She hadn't called the ambulance. Maybe a neighbor had seen or smelled smoke. Maybe someone had called the fire department. But she couldn't count on their getting in. Keep going. Keep going. At one point she slipped and slid down two steps, bumping her chin on a step. She grabbed an edge and hung on, stopping her forward motion.

"That's it, Megan. Hurry. Let Robert in. He'll help you."

Robert? Of course, it was Robert at the door. Robert would help her. He was worried, so worried. She lay at the bottom of the stairs, exhausted. She shivered as the cold of the flagstone entry seeped into the palms of her hands, her cheeks. The pounding started again.

Sliding to the door, she pulled herself to her knees and twisted at the knob of the massive oak door. She fell backward as Robert pushed it open.

"Megan. Megan! Are you all right? Oh, Megan." He gathered her into his arms. Megan felt the dampness of melted snow on his coat, then the warmth of his lips on her cold face. Quickly, he began to untie her wrists while her father untied her feet.

"Megan, my God. What happened to you?" Mr. Davidson asked. "Who did this to you?"

"Derrick. Oh, Daddy, in the living room. Get Mrs. Ames. Hurry. The fire . . ."

Mr. Davidson rushed past them as Robert helped Megan to her feet. "Can you walk, Megan? Are you all right?"

"I—I think so. The pictures . . . I feel better now." She coughed again, but breathed in the cold, frosty air from the doorway gratefully.

"She's not in there, Megan. Do you think she's in the house?"

"Yes, I'm sure. I'm sure she is. She's in the other bedroom, Daddy. Derrick took her there. Hurry." Megan looked up. Flames snapped and crackled from the top floor. Thick, black smoke was coming down the stairway. "No." Megan grabbed her father's arm as he started to climb the stairway. "You can't go. It's too late." Her father started upstairs despite her pleading. Megan screamed.

"Let him try, Megan. Let's get outside." Robert pulled Megan out of the house, and they stumbled across the street. He asked a neighbor to call the fire department. Megan couldn't stay inside and wait. Wrapped in a blanket the neighbor provided, she stood in the snow and watched Derrick's front door. She didn't have to worry for long. Her father stumbled out of the house coughing.

"Daddy, Daddy." Megan ran to him. "I was so afraid for you."

"I couldn't get up there, Megan. I went to the kitchen and soaked a towel in water to put over my face. But it was useless. The smoke is too thick and the fire has spread quickly. It seems to be coming from two directions, as if it started from both sides of the house."

Apparently Derrick hadn't relied on the fire in the darkroom being enough. He had started another fire in his mother's bedroom after taking her there.

"Let's get you home, Megan," Robert urged. "I know the police will want to talk to you, but they can come to the house later."

Megan told them her story after her father had treated the abrasions on her face and legs and wrists. Robert filled her full of hot tea. She shivered again, however, thinking she wouldn't feel warm or safe for a long time.

"When you weren't home, I called the school." Mr. Davidson explained how Robert had come to their house. "Since the TV was on, I looked all over. I couldn't believe you'd gone out."

"Fortunately, I guessed where you'd gone," Robert said. "Oh, Megan, why did you take such a chance?" Robert kept holding Megan's hand, as if he couldn't believe she was safe.

"No one would believe me, Robert. I had to know. And I would have still been—sick, if I hadn't gone there. He'd still have the pictures. You wouldn't believe that Derrick was causing all this. My illness, all of the sickness."

"Megan," her father said after listening to the whole story. He sat at the kitchen table with her. "Megan, baby, do you think anyone will believe you, even now? They'll believe that Derrick is sick, very sick, to do this to you. But to believe that his camera was—well, was taking your soul—your life, no one—"

"You don't believe it, even now, do you, Daddy?"

"I don't know. I just can't—I don't know. I know you appeared to be ill . . . that Cynthia is dead. I guess I'd prefer to think it was a virus, some germ, and that the connection with Derrick was a coincidence."

The tape recorder. Megan patted her pocket. Gone. Where was it? Somewhere in Derrick's house. What was left of his house. It must have fallen from her pocket when she fell to the floor or crawled . . . She sighed.

"Then you both think I shouldn't tell the police the whole story—the camera part? You think they'd laugh at me?"

"Probably. The newspapers would print it—they'd love it, but . . ."

"Everyone would think I was crazy too?" Megan looked at Robert and her father. They loved her. They wanted to believe. But if *they* didn't . . . couldn't . . . "Okay, we'll just say that Derrick was ill. But when they find him, what about the camera?"

"Let's wait and see. Maybe we can think of some way to destroy it. Just in case." Robert smiled at her.

"Do you think the police will find him, Robert?"

"Of course they will, Megan. I don't understand how he thought he'd get away with killing you, and his mother."

"I wasn't supposed to have escaped, Robert. It was supposed to have looked like an accident. Like his mother started the fire—when she was drunk. And somehow I was trapped there. In the fire." Megan shuddered again.

"It's okay, Megan. You're safe now." Robert hugged her tightly.

"Dad, will you call the hospital? See if Bunny and Roxie are better. If they are—"

"If they are, we'll be glad. Okay?" Megan's father smiled and kissed her.

While her dad made the call, Robert and Megan moved into the family room and started a fire. Just looking at it, though, hearing the snap and crackle, made Megan shiver. Fire no longer had the friendly warmth it had earlier today.

"Megan, when this is over, will you promise me you'll go back to reporting the news, not acting it out?" Robert kissed Megan's cheek, pulled her close to him. She leaned into the warmth and safety of his shoulder.

"I'll try, Robert. Believe me, I'm more comfortable in that role. I won't relax until they find Derrick, though. And I may never feel the same way about having my picture taken. Or even of taking photographs myself."

Megan's dad reported back that Bunny and Roxie were much improved. They were planning to go home from the hospital tomorrow. Megan felt glad, but it only reinforced her belief in the part of the story that would go untold. Was she right in withholding all the facts—the evidence, circumstantial as it was? She couldn't help but feel that some harm would come by her keeping quiet.

# Epilogue

A few days later, some miles away—a little over a thousand, to be exact—a yellow van pulled into a real estate office. Warren Groober was delighted to see a customer, any customer, even one so young. Times were hard, and he hadn't had a sale for months. He was disappointed that the young man wanted only a rental property, but perked up when he saw three months' rent in advance.

"Yes, sir. That's a fine location you've picked out, young man. What business did you say you were in? Altman, you said your name was?" Beat-up van, but at least he wasn't dressed like the vagrants that usually drove those things. His curly hair was cut short and his glasses made him look serious.

"Yes, sir. David Altman. I'm a photographer."

Funny little smile. Quiet feller, but polite. "Well, you've come to the right state. We have some of the most beautiful women in the South right here."

"Yes, sir. I saw the sign. Miss America."

"Sign? Oh, yeah. I remember seeing on the TV that they put that billboard up last year. Home of Miss America. We're right proud of that. Yes sirree, if you want to photograph Southern beauties, you've come to the right place. My daughter's a cheer-leader. She's as pretty as a picture, if I do say so myself."

"I'm sure she is."

"She'll be needing a picture for the annual soon. Lots of the best-looking girls last year went clear to Little Rock to get a good photograph. If you're any good, they won't have to do that this year, Mr. Altman."

"My photos are very professional, Mr. Groober. I'm sure they'll be happy with them. And as a favor to you, I'll give your daughter a free sitting."

"Well, that's right nice of you. I'm sure SueAnne will be plumb tickled. She does love getting her picture taken. You know how pretty girls are." Warren Groober laughed and winked at the young man.

"Yes, I know, Mr. Groober. I know. Makes my work easy. Tell her I'll be open by Saturday and to bring her friends."

"I'll do that. Now you take care, you hear?" Warren Groober watched the young man leave. Young feller, but serious. Not at all smart-alecky like some his age. He looked at the flier announcing the new business and thought of the free picture-taking session. SueAnne would be plumb tickled all right. Warren knew she would. Ever since she was little she had dearly loved having her picture taken.

BARBARA STEINER has photographed people, places, and animals in Africa, India, Australia, Russia, China, and Mongolia. Traveling is her number-one hobby, but she also likes tennis, backpacking, and square dancing. She has two daughters and lives in Boulder, Colorado, with two cats. She has written many books for young people, but this is her first novel of the supernatural.

## Avon Flare Mysteries
### by Edgar Award-Winning Author

# JAY BENNETT

**THE DEATH TICKET**  89597-8/$2.95 US/$3.50 Can

Trouble arrives when a lottery ticket turns up a winner—worth over six million dollars—and maybe more than one life!

**THE EXECUTIONER**  79160-9/$2.95 US/3.95 Can

Indirectly responsible for a friend's death, Bruce is consumed by guilt—until someone is out to get *him*.

## And Spine-tingling Suspense
### from the author of *Slumber Party*

# CHRISTOPHER PIKE

**CHAIN LETTER**  89968-X/$3.50 US/$4.25 Can

One by one, the chain letter was coming to each of them ...demanding dangerous, impossible deeds. None in the group wanted to believe it—until the accidents—and the dying—started happening!